The Rabbit's Hole

By
Brian Christopher
SHEA

The Rabbit's Hole is a work of fiction. Any names, characters, places, and incidents are the product of the author's imagination or are used fictitiously. Any resemblance to actual persons, living or dead, events, or locales is entirely coincidental.

Copyright © 2018 Brian Christopher Shea all rights reserved.

www.brianchristophershea.com

info@brianchristophershea.com

JOIN MY READER LIST:
https://brianchristophershea.com/contact/

No part of this publication may be reproduced, transmitted, or transmitted in any form or by any means, including photocopying, recording or other electronic or mechanical methods, without the prior written permission of the publisher, except in the case of brief quotations embodied in reviews and certain other non-commercial uses permitted by copyright law.

ISBN: 9781731417893

Author Photograph by Adam Rembisz
https://www.instagram.com/adam_blaise

Editor: Dana Lee:
https://www.lee-clarityconsulting.com

Cover design by Momir Borocki
momir.borocki@gmail.com

The Nick Lawrence Series:

Book One:
The Camel's Back

Book Two:
The Lion's Mouth

Book Three:
The Rabbit's Hole

Book Four:
The Wolf's Door
(Coming March 2019)

Chapter 1

His eyes flickered, allowing the meager light of the room to filter in. He lay on his back looking up as the yellow and brown circles of the water-damaged ceiling came into focus. An unwelcome combination of cigarette smoke and wet dog clung to the damp air. He tried sitting up but couldn't. Nothing. His body was locked in place. Panic set in at the sudden realization that his arms and legs were tightly bound. The fibers of the rag stuffed in his mouth tickled the back of his throat. The gag made it impossible to speak. He closed his eyes hard willing himself to wake from this wretched dream.

His eyes opened again. To his dismay, he was still in the dimly lit room. His arms strained against their restraints. A muffled scream seeped out through the cloth in his mouth. He writhed. The only part of his body that wasn't tied down was his head. He tried to calm himself and take a look around. His heart pounded, and he started hyperventilating. Unable to get enough oxygen through his nose, he breathed hard through the cloth in his mouth. This only made things worse as more of the gag was forced deeper into his mouth and his lungs pulled hard. A wheezing hum bubbled up from his throat. He swung his head from side to side searching desperately for an answer to this nightmare. It was hard to tell from the dull light that framed the drab curtain whether it was day or night. To the right was another bed and beyond that he could make out a small round table and chair by another window. There was something familiar about this place, but in his current state he couldn't clear his mind enough to place it.

A clang. The sound of something hard against porcelain. Its distinctive sound caused him to look left, hoping to find the source. He found nothing but a wall. His gaze followed the faded floral wallpaper toward an opening where he could see the corner of a sink and an open closet. One thing he was certain of was that he was definitely in a motel room. How he got here was another question. His mind raced, searching for the answer.

The sound again, clang. Light flooded into the room from the opening to his left. His eyes were still adjusting to its introduction when a shadow crept across the floor as if chasing the light away, and his panic rose. He shook the bindings on his wrists and ankles hard. It did nothing to loosen him from the confines of the bed. With each pull and twist of his body the shackles cut deeper into his flesh.

A figure emerged from behind the wall where he assumed the bathroom was located and stood at edge of the bed. He strained to see anything that would provide an answer to this hellish situation. The figure's head cocked ever so slightly to the left, evaluating him. He couldn't make out any facial features. The figure standing before him looked black as night.

A flash drew his attention down to the figure's right hand. The bathroom light reflected off the shiny surface of a large knife. He screamed but through the cloth it came out as a whimper. The figure moved quickly across the room. A click, and the television came to life. The images of an old black and white war movie filled in the backdrop behind the dark figure. The sounds of planes and bombs muted any chance of him being heard from a neighboring guest.

The figure approached and leaned in. He now understood why he couldn't discern any features. The face, now only inches away, was shrouded by a tightly fitted black mask. What was even stranger was that a pair of sunglasses with red tinted lenses covered its eyes. In the strange desperation of the moment, the glasses reminded him of a combination of Jim Morrison and the devil.

The figure cocked its head again. He followed the shadowed movement over to the table by the window. The figure returned with the rickety wooden chair and sat. The knife now rested on the nightstand only inches from his face. A constant reminder of his dire circumstances.

"There is a reckoning upon you," the masked figure said.

The voice sent a chill down the man's spine. The voice was deep and had a robotic hiss that followed the statement.

"I know you. I know what you've done. The courts will fail you. They won't do justice for the horrible crimes that you've committed." The boom and hiss of each word resonated in the helpless man's ears.

"In a perfect world you would be brutalized in the same way that you've brutalized others. But our world isn't perfect. And thus, I am here."

The imprisoned man twisted, trying to escape. His shoulders almost came out of their sockets. The bite from his right wrist's restraint now released a slow trickle of blood. He could feel the warm liquid rolling steadily down his hand and off the tip of his pinky finger.

"Are you still trying to figure out how you got here?"

The man on the bed nodded vigorously.

"Think."

The man on the bed cocked an eyebrow and squinted hard, trying to see through the rose-colored glasses of his captor. Something familiar in the eyes. His thought was interrupted as the masked figure sat back and withdrew a black handgun from his waistline. The weapon was placed next to the knife. The darkness of it was in stark contrast to the glint of the blade.

"They didn't have a choice. But you do." The metallic rasp of the voice carried with it an added weight.

The man on the bed craned his neck and eyed the weapons on the nightstand. His vision blurred as his eyes started to water, and he blinked rapidly to clear the tears. Bombs and the staccato of rapid-fire machine gun blasts poured from the television in the backdrop. The man on the bed looked away, facing his head toward the wall.

A gloved hand gripped his lower jaw firmly and turned his head back to the intense stare of the eyes hiding behind the rose-colored glasses. He resisted, but the effort was futile. The bastard must be deriving some sick pleasure out of this. Maybe even smiling?

"What's your choice?"

The man on the bed screamed again. His jugular engorged with blood at the strain of his futile efforts.

The figure in the chair slowly tapped a gloved finger back and forth between the two weapons. The man slowly and desperately shook his head and pleaded with his eyes.

"Life or death is not your choice. Death is inevitable. It's the how that you get to decide. Tick tock."

The man began a rhythmic shaking of his head and his body quivered involuntarily.

"There is no fixing what you are. There is no justice that will undo what you've done."

The words were *spoken more softly*, but the finality in the message was clear. The gloved hand continued to move back and forth between the weapons metronomically.

"Know this. Your death will be far less painful than the lives of the people you've hurt. I can see that you're incapable of deciding. That's okay. I will lift that burden for you."

At the same moment, the man on the bed widened his eyes in sudden recognition of the masked person seated before him. He finally connected the dots. He wept silently, choking on the mucus that rolled to the back of his throat. Once again, tears blurred his vision, but this time he didn't bother to try to clear them. His breath whistled out of his nose, a long soft-noted sigh. Then all resistance faded, and his body went slack. The man on the bed closed his eyes, knowing that he would never open them again.

Chapter 2

"Are you ready?" Anaya asked.

"If you mean packed, then yes," Nick said.

"What's your worry? This is going to be fun."

"I know, it's just that I don't know if we're interfering. You know it's been almost six months? Maybe she doesn't want us to come."

Anaya giggled. "Are you kidding me? She's been blowing up my phone all morning long."

"What about her new family? Maybe they're not ready for us. Maybe we're a reminder that she wasn't always theirs?" Nick questioned.

"Did you feel that way? Were you worried that finding your biological parents would've disrupted the family who raised you?"

"No. But then again I was never able to locate them."

"If you had, do you think your parents would've been upset?" Anaya asked.

"I don't think so. I know that my mom was a bit ambivalent. Maybe she worried that I'd like them better or something."

"Probably just a mother's worry. Adopted or not, you were her son. I could see that being unsettling."

"Yeah I know. That's the funny thing about being adopted. No matter how much everyone tells you that you belong, there's always a part that just feels lost," Nick said.

"My bouncing through the foster care system was definitely different from the stability your parents gave you after adoption. That's why I pulled some strings to guarantee Mouse would be placed in a family that wouldn't spit her back after six months," Anaya said.

Nick stuffed the plastic confines of his suitcase haphazardly without much regard for his clothes. He closed it. The suitcase was at max capacity. Nick placed both hands on the top, leaned forward, and applied the weight of his muscular frame, compressing the contents. He finagled his hand to the zipper and tugged.

The pull tab nimbly balanced in his finger dragged the slider around the expanse, following the path of teeth chugging along like the little engine that could.

Secured, Nick stepped back to appreciate his work. He caught Anaya out of the corner of his eye. Her arms were folded, and her head shook. Nick couldn't tell if it was a look of amazement or admonishment.

Anaya giggled. It was lighthearted and giddy. "For someone who spent the early part of their adult life packing and carrying rucksacks, I am amazed at the struggle that I just witnessed."

"It was a simpler time," Nick said, reciprocating the laugh.

Anaya handed him the boarding passes she'd printed for their six o'clock flight. Nick took them and slipped them into his travel bag, a blue Jansport that contained a spare set of clothes, book, and a toothbrush.

"I still can't believe that you were able to get her placed in Pidgeon, Michigan. Talk about keeping a promise. You're pretty amazing Ms. Patel."

"Plus, the Westons are great people. They knew what they were getting into when they took on Mouse. This isn't their first rodeo," Anaya said deflecting the compliment.

"I guess I was just nervous. I don't have much experience with kids besides trying to save them from predators. I hope she still thinks I'm cool," Nick said.

"I don't think she ever did. So, you don't have to worry about that."

Nick relaxed as Anaya slid her hand across his back. Her fingers lingered over the small lumps of scar tissue on his shoulder, the ever-present reminder of his time overseas. Three rounds from an enemy rifle that had almost cost him his life. His body was a tapestry of *almosts*.

Her caress stirred him, causing him to turn and face her. Anaya's deep brown eyes caught the light accentuating the yellow flecks that peppered her pupils. Her beauty gave him pause. She smiled looking up at Nick. Her arms draped around his neck and their lips met.

"Get your head out of your ass Nicholas Lawrence. This is going to be a great trip," Anaya said as she buried her head into his neck.

"I love when you take charge."

"God knows you need it. I think you'd still be hemming and hawing on whether to ask me out if I'd left things in your hands," Anaya said, still pressing her face gently against him.

Nick chuckled softly. "I'm glad you didn't."

He smiled and pushed her silky black hair across her bronzed shoulder. Leaning in, he kissed the warmth of her exposed neck, tasting a hint of the cocoa butter lotion she moisturized herself with each morning.

Anaya gave a coy smile. An urgency lay just beneath the surface of her playfulness. "I was going to wait, but I figure now is as good a time as any."

"Wait for what?" Nick asked.

Anaya released her gentle embrace and stepped back from him.

Nick watched as she walked out of their bedroom. He'd abandoned his apartment after his near fatal encounter, and the two took a leap of faith, making the decision to move in together. Life moved a little faster when you were older. They had found a small ranch-styled home near the picturesque downtown area of Georgetown. The bedroom was a work in progress and much of their stuff was still in boxes. He surveyed his new life and smiled.

She returned a short time later with her hands behind her back. Anaya had a wide grin that seemed to spread wide beyond the boundaries of her face.

Nick panicked and looked at his watch, trying without success to match the date to some significant event. "Did I forget some anniversary?"

Anaya swayed with her head cocked, looking up at him through her long eyelashes. "No. Not yet."

"Well you've got me stumped," Nick said defeatedly.

"The master investigator can't read my facial clues? I'm shocked," Anaya said sarcastically.

Nick watched as Anaya closed the distance slowly. He could tell she really enjoyed tormenting him. He shook his head in mock frustration. Anaya stepped close and revealed her hands. In them lay a small wrapped gift. The shiny silver paper framed by the sepia of her palms.

Nick cocked an eyebrow of suspicion. "Oh boy." Nick sighed.

Anaya said nothing. She waited eagerly, rocking back and forth in anticipation as Nick tore through the silver wrapping paper.

Nick looked down at the white 5x7 frame in his hand. He squinted, peering down at the black and white image encased beneath the thin layer of glass.

His jaw went slack, and he looked up at the woman standing in front of him. The yellow flecks in her eyes seemed to dance as they welled up with tears. Nick felt a warmth spread over his cheeks. His eyes blurred, and a smile stretched. He dropped down on his knees and hugged Anaya tightly around her waist. Nick pulled her into him, pressing his lips against her stomach.

"How far along?" Nick asked.

"The doctor said eight weeks."

"When did you find out?"

"Last week," Anaya said.

"Last week?" Nick asked pulling back and looking up into Anaya's eyes, still wet with tears.

"I knew something was off, and so I took a home pregnancy test. I wanted to be sure before I told you. So, I went to the doctor," Anaya paused exhaling deeply. "I was so worried. I didn't know how you were going to react. Things were moving fast, and this just puts us into overdrive."

Nick slumped to the ground, looking at the picture again. His eyes traced the grainy lines that defined the life that was growing inside the woman before him.

"This is the best day of my life." Nick's voice cracked as he spoke. The sound of it caught him off guard.

Anaya wiped her face and looked down at Nick with a seriousness he didn't normally see. "I don't want you to feel trapped. It's still just us. No need to run off and get married."

"Married. We should—I mean when. We've—um—never really talked about—," Nick mumbled almost incoherently.

Anaya pressed her finger against his lips, silencing him.

"It's okay. We'll figure everything out in due time. Right now, we've got to get ready for our flight," Anaya whispered.

"Flight. Can you travel? Did you ask the doctor?" Nick asked. He felt lost and immediately overwhelmed. Two feelings that Nick was unaccustomed to.

"Yes, I asked, and he said it's fine. Nothing to worry about this early in the pregnancy."

"Do we know if it's a boy or girl?" Nick asked.

"That's at next month's visit," Anaya said rubbing his head.

"I'm so excited. I should call someone. Maybe Declan or Jones?"

"How about we wait? The doctor said it's best to hold off until we get past the first trimester. You'll have to hold on for about one more month," Anaya said, patting Nick's head. "Do you think you can do that?"

"Maybe we could tell Mouse?" Nick said.

"Okay, only Mouse. I never realized how bad you are at keeping secrets." Anaya smiled and reached out her hands.

Nick nodded, taking her outstretched hands, allowing her to assist him up from the floor. *Bad at keeping secrets*, he thought. A pang of guilt struck him, knowing Anaya had no idea how wrong she was.

Chapter 3

The temperature had dropped over the night and sealed the windows in icy fractals that, under other circumstances, might've been considered beautiful. Not so pretty when you're running late and can't see out your window.

Izzy Martinez had spent the last ten minutes letting her silver Elantra defrost. She'd forgotten to put her wiper blades up the night before and they were frozen in place to the front windshield. Izzy went back in to warm herself and make a cup of coffee for the road. She had an early meeting in New Haven. There had been whispers that she would be taking the lead on a major investigation. Her heart rate accelerated at the thought. She'd been involved with big cases, but never led a team. She exhaled the anticipation, her breath visible as she exited the warmth of her modest condo.

Armed with the knowledge that icy roads would make for a slower than normal commute, she decided to leave earlier than usual. Izzy stepped carefully, gingerly navigating the slick walkway out to the parking lot. She cradled her favorite stainless steel mug as she entered the car.

The windshield didn't look much better than it had before. She rummaged under the seats looking for the scraper, mad at herself for not cleaning her car at the end of the season. Her house was tidy, but the Hyundai not so much. She blew a sigh of relief at finding the mitten covered grip. Izzy looked at the dash display. The outside temperature was a balmy 18 degrees Fahrenheit. She took a long draw from the travel mug and allowed the hot liquid to add a barrier of internal warmth before stepping back into the cold.

"I should've stayed in Texas with Nick," Izzy said aloud. *Great, now I'm talking to myself,* she thought. One of the many signs of insanity.

The thought of Nick made her stop, hand on the door handle. The last time she'd talked to him was almost six months ago. It may as well have been forever. Why now? Why at the butt crack of dawn in the tundra of an unprecedented early onset of a formidable New England winter?

She let the thought of Nick dissipate as she pushed the door open. A fierce wind swept in forcefully, nearly slamming the door into her face. She won the battle against the gale and buried her face in the high zippered collar of her fleece-lined parka. The FBI spent lots of money on useless gadgetry but seemed to come up short when it came to cold weather gear. The cold air penetrated the layers of clothing within seconds of Izzy's exit from the car. Her teeth chattered uncontrollably as she scraped like a madwoman at the ice. Bits of cold shards sprayed into her face, causing her to take on a frenzied look.

Satisfied that the window was cleared enough to drive, she climbed back into the car. Seated and shivering, Izzy pressed her fingers against the vents allowing the warm air to thaw their rigidity. A few minutes passed before mobility returned. It was at times like these that she kicked herself for not taking an assignment in Florida.

She gripped the steering wheel and began backing out of her parking space. She could see the fluffy white tail of her cat, Mr. Tippins, wag his goodbye. He was always perched on the couch set against the window. Sadly, he was the only male to stick around in her life.

Izzy made her way out of her condo complex and toward the nearby entrance ramp to I-91 South.

The entrance ramp had a slight incline and the weathered tires of the Elantra slipped on the black ice before regaining their purchase with a dry patch of asphalt. The slight skidding reminded her that she was overdue for snow tires. Izzy made a mental note to schedule an appointment with the tire shop once she got into the office.

She was right to leave early. It wasn't long before she was stuck in bumper-to-bumper traffic moving at a snail's pace. The sun wouldn't be up for another hour, but it appeared that other commuters had the same idea to beat the rush hour. Her mind drifted as she sat idling behind a never-ending line of brake lights. Her thoughts were of Nick.

Izzy took out her cell phone. A couple taps on the screen and she was staring at Nick's number. Too early to call. *To text or not to text, that is the question.* She'd faced this internal battle too many times to count in the last few months. Her stubborn nature had always won out.

Today, maybe due to the cold or early morning fatigue, or a combination of the two, she caved.

The screen glowed and was brighter in the comparative darkness of the early morning. She looked down at the blinking curser taunting her to begin tapping her message. What do you say to someone you love but haven't spoken to in half a year?

Her thumb hovered briefly in its last moment of resistance before beginning an assaultive fury of the digital keyboard. Izzy's thoughts poured out onto the screen like prisoners released prior to a death sentence.

Why didn't you choose me? Why did you let me walk away? I've been waiting for you to figure it out. I've been waiting for you to tell me you love me. I can't wait anymore. I'll say it if you're too weak. I love you! Her mind shouted the words, but her thumb nimbly navigated the keyboard delivering a veiled conveyance of her thoughts. Her thumb stopped moving. It hovered again, this time above the send button like it had many times before. She would not erase the words. This time would be different. At least if she sent it her mind would be at ease.

She heard it before she saw it. The crunch of metal. It sounded like an explosion. Jolted from her thoughts Izzy looked up, dropping her phone as the headlights of an eighteen-wheeler filled her view, blinding her.

The massive front end of the truck collided with the Jersey barrier. The concrete stopped the truck, but the impact swung the trailer portion hard. The bang of the truck's initial crash gave way to a loud creaking noise as the jackknifed trailer shot up into the air and over the short wall of the concrete partition. The approaching rectangular container hung in the air as if deciding which way to fall. It seemed to be moving in slow motion, and Izzy could read the words Tommy D's Plumbing Supplies shrink wrapped on the ribbed siding of the metallic box. The momentary pause ended and the towering mass hurtled downward, toward her.

Izzy looked for an avenue to escape. She was boxed in, the concrete barrier to her left and pinned on the other three sides by commuters. She gunned the accelerator. Her bald tires spun hard on the icy road causing her to fish tail. She spun into the car on her right. Her Elantra pressed hard into a Prius. Wedged together, both vehicles were no longer able to move. Other drivers began reacting to the impending collision. Horns blared, and a mad game of bumper cars ensued.

The bright light of the eighteen-wheeler suddenly disappeared, and Izzy was encased in the looming shadow of the falling trailer. Izzy was slammed facedown into the passenger seat. Unable to move, a searing pain radiated from the center of her back. Her feet tingled and then suddenly felt as if they were on fire. Her face pressed between the soft upholstery and the hard metal of the roof. She tasted blood. Izzy quickly found that she was only able to take short breaths as an immense weight pressed down hard.

Enveloped in a shroud of fear. Trapped in the dark, the only glimmer of light came from the flickering cellphone screen mocking her with the unsent message to Nick.

With each exhale, the crushed metal of the roof cinched tighter, making every breath in shallower than the one before. The pain in her legs was initially excruciating. And then the agony was replaced by a nothingness.

The nothingness was bad. Izzy inhaled some of the blood that was trickling into her mouth, causing her to cough. The metal of the roof dug into her neck.

Izzy tried wiggling her hand free. Nothing. Her hands did not respond to command. She felt nothing below the neck. This was bad, really bad.

She blinked her left eye rapidly as blood from an unseen wound leaked into the corner. Izzy closed it, trying, without success, to keep the blood out.

Her breathing became more ragged and desperate. Izzy's right eye began to close. She fought to stay awake, willing herself to live.

Chapter 4

Anaya gave her infectious giggle. "Are you already eating for two?"

"I'm just trying to show my support of the airport food industry. I can't pass up a soft pretzel opportunity," Nick said as he popped a salty bite into his mouth. "I know, I'm weak. It's my kryptonite."

"I now understand why you've never complained about all your job-related travels. It's because you've been having an affair with Auntie Annie."

"Guilty as charged." Nick grinned, his cheeks puffed out like a chipmunk storing nuts for the winter.

A three-toned chime rang out over the public announcement system. A reminder to notify police if a bag is left unattended. It was the third time he'd heard it in a very short period of time. Nick knew that broadcasts like these weren't a deterrent to a serious attack. He'd seen the commitment first hand of those on that path. These messages served a different purpose that few in the population realized. They were designed to give travelers the impression of safety. It was psychologically calming to think that everyone in earshot of the message would vigilantly identify a threat. It also gave the masses the sense that they had some power to stop it. Sadly, Nick knew the reality and so to him that loud, repetitive mantra of the TSA announcement just added annoyance, interrupting the salty deliciousness of his last bite of pretzel.

"This is a great thing we're doing. Look how happy she is," Anaya said, looking at the screen of her cell phone.

Anaya opened the most recent chain of messages and scrolled down to the image. Nick leaned to his left, peering over her shoulder at the picture of Mouse holding a golden-brown puppy.

"Looking at her there and thinking back to what she looked like when we first found her, it's like she's not even the same person," Nick said.

Anaya sat back, closed her eyes, and nestled her head on his shoulder. She sighed, rubbing her tummy. "A lot's changed since that day."

Nick chuckled. "A lot's changed since this morning."

His phone buzzed, and he shifted to retrieve it from his front pocket, making a concerted effort not to displace Anaya's head.

"It's Declan. Should I answer?" Nick asked.

"Absolutely. We've still got another forty minutes until we board. You two boys need to catch up, but remember our little secret," Anaya said with a wink.

Nick stood and kissed Anaya on the head before walking to a less populated section of the gate area. He leaned against a cylindrical pillar and looked out at the choreographed maneuvers of the ground personal as they directed the movements of the planes arriving and departing. It was a masterful blend of training and execution.

Nick answered just before the call went to voicemail. "Hey buddy, this is a nice surprise. And to what do I owe this honor?"

Nick didn't hear a response from his normally verbose friend. He only heard a muffled sigh.

"Declan? Are you there?"

"Um yeah, sorry. I've got some bad news," Declan said softly.

Hearing Declan Enright at a loss for words had Nick worried, but he tried not to let it show. "Best to just say it, plain and straight. Not much left in this world that shocks me anymore."

"It's Izzy. She's hurt real bad. ICU."

"What? How?" Nick stammered.

"Car accident early this morning. She's been in and out of surgery. I just got the call. Val and I are heading that way now."

"Level with me, how bad are we talking?" Nick asked.

"Too early to tell, but from what I do know is that it's critical. If she pulls through, it's unlikely that she'll walk again."

Nick's body went limp. The pillar now supported all of his weight as he used it as a crutch. He looked over at Anaya. She must've noticed the distress on his face because she mouthed "everything okay?" Nick held up one finger, gesturing for her to hold on a minute. It felt like a rude gesture, but Nick needed to gather himself.

"What did you mean by *if she makes it?*"

"All I have right now is that there is a fifty percent chance that she may not come out of the next surgery. She's been unconscious since they brought her in."

"You said car accident?" Nick asked.

"Yeah. From what I understand, an eighteen-wheeler lost control and rolled over the median into Izzy's lane. There are already two dead, including the truck driver. Like I said, it's bad." Declan cleared his throat. "Once I'm at the hospital I'll know more."

"Keep me posted when you hear anything. I'm in the airport about to fly out to see Mouse."

"Shit that's right. Today is the big trip. Damn. I hate to be the bearer of bad news." Declan paused, and his voice took on a more optimistic tone. "Izzy's as tough as they come. I'm sure she's going to pull through. She'll be in the hospital for a long while. You go with Anaya, and I'll keep you posted. Maybe you can make a trip this way when you get back?"

"I'll figure it out. I want constant updates, and I want a call as soon as she's out of surgery! If I'm in the air, then leave me a message."

"Will do. Gotta go. Say hi to Mouse for me," Declan said, and the phone call ended.

Nick pocketed the phone and slowly trudged his way back to Anaya. He avoided eye contact, fearing that it would betray his devastation. He sat without saying a word as he worked hard to process the information he'd just received.

"So are you going to tell me what that was all about?" Anaya asked.

"Izzy's hurt bad," Nick blurted.

Nick felt Anaya tense at the mention of her name. It was slight, and most people wouldn't have noticed, but when it came to his ability to detect the imperceptible reactions in others, Nick was not like most people.

Anaya had confronted him, only once, about his feelings for his former partner. Nick had minimized any relationship, but he knew that Anaya saw through it. She never pressed him again on the issue, but any mention of her name brought an awkward tension between the two of them. It was usually brief but always present, and Nick felt it now.

"Job related?" Anaya asked.

Nick shook his head slowly. "Car accident."

"How bad?"

"Declan said she may not pull through."

"Jesus. What do you want to do?" Anaya said taking his hand.

"Not much I can do. We're about to fly out to Michigan for a mini vacation." Nick said in a tone more snarky than he intended and immediately regretted it.

"This trip is more than a vacation and you know that," Anaya shot back.

"I know. That came out wrong. I'm just a bit overwhelmed."

Nick leaned forward placing his elbows on his knees. He let his face fall into the palms of his hands. He rubbed at the lines of stress etched into his brow.

"You didn't let me finish. Izzy's circumstance trumps this trip without question. You need to go see your friend."

"What are you saying?" Nick asked, peeking out at Anaya.

"I'm saying get your ass up out of that seat, go to the ticket counter, and book a damn flight to Connecticut!" Anaya said, sounding like a drill sergeant motivating a fresh recruit.

"But this trip is something we've been planning for months. I know how important it is—for us and Mouse."

"I'll go to Mouse. You go to Izzy."

Nick noticed Anaya purse her lips at the mention of her name. He knew that her decision, although it came quickly, was not an easy one.

"What did I do to deserve you?" Nick asked.

"Just make sure you come back to me." Anaya paused, placing her hand across her belly. "To us."

Nick smiled weakly, leaned down, and kissed her. He glided his hand over hers. "I'll let you know as soon as I have a plan. Give Mouse a big hug for me."

"Nick, I really do hope that Izzy's all right."

Nick nodded. He gave Anaya one last kiss atop her head, breathing in deeply the subtle scent of lilacs, before he grabbed his backpack and headed off in the direction of the ticket counters. He looked back only once before disappearing in the disjointed flow of wayward travelers.

Chapter 5

Kemper Jones sat in his cubicle staring at the case files spread unevenly across his desk. He'd unbuttoned his pants in an effort to relieve the pressure. His khakis were now secured only by the worn leather of his belt with the buckle gripping desperately at the last notch, like a free climber holding on for dear life to the edge of a cliff.

His stomach rumbled loudly, and he looked at the clock. The diet he'd started was killing him. He was supposed to remain in a fasting state until noon. He eyed the wall clock that seemed to mock him with each jittery tick of its hand. Jones still had a few hours until he planned to take his lunch, but his hunger was definitely speeding up that timeline. He could always just start over tomorrow.

The heavyset detective from Austin Police Department's sex crimes unit drummed the beat of Journey's *Don't Stop Believing* into the closed manila folder in front of him, preparing to open it as his phone rang.

"Detective Jones," he said into the receiver, happy for the distraction from his pangs of hunger.

"Hey Kemper, it's Pete Cavanaugh. I got something I need your eyes on."

"Shit." Jones knew that it was never good when Homicide called. "How old is she?"

"Not a kid. Not even a girl," Cavanaugh said.

"Now I'm intrigued. What'ya got?" Jones asked with a thick drawl.

"It's best you come here."

Jones didn't respond. He felt the rumblings of a big case that was only rivaled by the rumbling in his empty stomach. His desire for burnt ends this early in the day had him concerned. *I'm an addict. Hi, my name is Kemper and I love barbeque.* Jones laughed to himself at the thought and envisioned himself speaking at a BBQ Anonymous meeting.

Jones redirected his attention to the man on the other end of the phone. He tapped the speaker function and set the phone on the disorganized pile that was his desktop. Jones removed his duty weapon from the top drawer of his file cabinet. He forced the pancake holster into place on his hip. The weight of the gun added to the precarious rigging of his pants and tested the tensile strength of his belt.

Cavanaugh was not a man to play games. The fact that he didn't want to talk about the scene was an indicator of bad things to come.

"Address?" Jones asked with an exasperated sigh, part exertion and part due to the foreboding of the unknown.

"The Stagecoach Inn."

"Why does that sound familiar?" Jones asked.

"Your big case," Cavanaugh said.

"Shit. Yup, you're right," Jones said kicking himself for not recalling it immediately. "You know how it goes, close the file and tuck it deep."

"Well you might want to open that file again," Cavanaugh said in a deep voice that conveyed the underlying seriousness of his statement.

Jones rubbed his temples with his thick, meaty fingers and closed his eyes for a moment.

"Room?"

"204."

"Double shit. I'm on the way."

Jones pulled up to the yellow police tape draped between two cruisers and a staircase railing, the hallmark of any bad scene. Guests and passerby foot traffic stopped in interest. The peering eyes of civilian onlookers always annoyed him. *Would knowing what lay inside the police boundary provide meaning to their lives?* If they knew, they'd never look. Maybe his anger stemmed from jealousy. He wished he could unsee many a scene. Man's ability to find new ways to inflict harm never ceased to amaze the seasoned detective.

Crowds sometimes gave an advantage to an investigator. In the sea of people, a potential *doer* occasionally returned to watch the madness of their crimes unfold. It was hard for them to let go of the perverse bond with the victim. Some had a deranged fascination with police investigations.

The heavyset detective scanned the crowd, looking for that set of eyes that was out of place. He searched the faces for a person who was absorbing the actions of the police.

Jones stretched as he exited the car. He pretended not to look at the group of people as he ducked under the tape. His incognito assessment of the crowd didn't trip any of his investigative alerts. Besides he knew one of the officers or crime scene techs would be tasked with photographing the group of onlookers for reference later.

It was cold by Austin standards but Jones's midriff bulk made the coat uncomfortably tight. He unzipped it and left it open, allowing for the icy wind to pass through. The effect was immediate and caused him to shiver slightly as he approached one of the patrol officers holding position on the perimeter.

"Cavanaugh?" Jones asked.

The young officer shrugged his shoulders and then pointed up to the second floor of the motel. "I'm guessing he'd be up there."

Jones nodded and walked toward the rust coated stairs of the rundown motel. The stairwell was outside and divided the complex down the middle.

He took each step deliberately, pacing his ascent. Jones didn't want to hit the second floor out of breath. He advanced toward a young female officer who stood frozen, staring wide-eyed into the motel room. Jones saw the lines of curiosity spiral across her supple skin. He guessed that this was probably one of the first big scenes she'd worked.

"Can you let Cavanaugh know that Jones is here?"

The young officer jumped at the sound of his voice. She flushed and tried to recover, looking down at the logbook tightly gripped in her cold hands.

She peeked her head into room 204. "Detective Cavanaugh, Detective Jones is here to see you."

"Well put him in the book and tell him to come in and join the party," Cavanaugh boomed from inside.

Jones initialed next to his entry time on the log and entered the all-too-familiar room. Cavanaugh was squatting awkwardly as he looked at the floor space between the two beds. His massive frame teetered like a boulder on a pebble.

The homicide detective stood as Jones entered. Cavanaugh's frame seemed even larger in the confined space of the cheap motel room. A former second round draft pick for the Dallas Cowboys, Cavanaugh had maintained his linebacker physique even though it'd been several years since he had stepped onto the gridiron.

"Been a while my friend," Cavanaugh said.

"That's because when our two worlds collide, it usually turns into a shitshow."

The large hand of Cavanaugh swallowed Jones's when he shook it.

"Let's get to it then."

Jones liked the point of fact method of communication from Cavanaugh. Cutting right to the chase was a good way to do business.

"A little ripe in here. Ever hear of fabreeze?" Jones asked, laughing at his own joke.

Cavanaugh chuckled.

"The call came in this morning. The room was paid in full for two nights. The maid came by after checkout to clean and that's when she noticed sleeping beauty over here."

Jones cracked a smile at the macabre reference. The sanity achieved through the dark humor of death investigators was often misunderstood.

"So why am I here? Seems like this case is outside of my wheelhouse. What am I missing?" Jones asked.

"Recognize the guy on the bed?"

"Not particularly." Jones looked at the body bound spread eagle on the bed. "If I met him before I don't recognize him. But then again I'm sure he didn't have hole in his head before either."

Cavanaugh laughed. "Richard Pentlow."

"Son of a bitch. I thought he was locked up awaiting trial on the rape of that eleven-year-old?" Jones asked, squinting his eyes at the dead man trying hard to remember what he looked like before the gunshot lobotomy.

"Nope. Released on bail three days ago."

"Looks like karma's a real bitch." Jones looked around the room, morbidly reminiscing about his last time in it. "This is the same room he abused that little girl in. Looks like someone didn't like it very much. In my humble opinion the world's a better place without him among the living."

"Couldn't agree more."

"I hope you don't break your back trying to find the killer. I would rather shake the guy's hand than slap the cuffs on him." Jones laid a thick west Texas drawl in this statement.

"That's the thing. Maybe you already have."

"Huh?" Jones asked, cocking a weary eyebrow.

Cavanaugh thumbed over his shoulder in the direction of the bathroom. The same bathroom where they'd rescued the group of young girls almost a year ago.

"Look at the mirror."

"Where the system fails I prevail." Jones read the big sloppy writing on the mirror hung between the bathroom and the open closet. Then along the bottom edge of the mirror Jones read silently, *Nick, what stands up tall but reaches low?*

"What kind of mumbo jumbo is that?" Jones asked.

"I thought maybe you could shed some light. Does the Nick reference mean anything to you?"

"It's gotta be Nick Lawrence. He and I partnered up on the case. Bureau guy."

"It's obvious the guy who did this knew about Pentlow's arrest, but more importantly knew about him being released on bail. The message at the bottom is also very concerning."

"That's a pretty big net you're casting. Maybe his wife? Or maybe the traffickers tying up loose ends?" Jones questioned.

"Yeah, could be."

"Seems like you don't much like my thoughts on the matter. Care to enlighten me?"

"It feels more like vigilante justice than an angry wife or organized crime hit." Cavanaugh said.

Cavanaugh was standing next to Jones. Through the smudged reflection of the mirror, the broad shoulders and slim waistline of the homicide detective made Jones feel even more portly than usual. As if on cue, his stomach made an audible rumble. His internal lunch whistle was blowing hard.

"Blood?" Jones asked, pointing at the writing on the mirror.

"Yup. It looks like he used Pentlow's to pen his poetry. We won't be certain until we hear back from the lab, but it's a good guess."

"So who's our vigilante?"

"That's the reason I wanted you to come down here. Maybe you could shed some light on this."

"Me? Why?" Jones asked.

"Well you worked the case. Maybe you got a feel for someone that took the investigation a little too personally."

Jones leaned in. His voice was intense but he kept his volume low so that the other investigator and crime scene techs didn't hear. "Hold up, you're asking me if I think a cop did this?"

"I'm not saying that. I'm just saying we've got to look at all the possibilities. That is one theory that's been kicked around, and one that I need to examine."

"Be careful throwing that around. The wrong person catches wind and we'll have a media shit storm," Jones said.

"I know. I'm keeping that one close." Cavanaugh paused, raising his eyebrows. "So what do you think?"

"I guess anything is possible. I'd be hard pressed to name anyone who was angered to the point of taking the law into their own hands. It was a bad case, but Pentlow was at the bottom rung of a much bigger problem."

"Okay let me ask it a different way. Do you think that anyone investigating the case seemed more affected?"

"It's a child rape case. Those hit everyone hard. Another girl was stabbed and left to die alone at the Hope Graffiti Park." Jones stopped talking. The memory of the little girl still woke him from sleep. Some deaths haunt, and that one had more than most. He shook off the thought. "But like I said, Pentlow was a pedophile but the group that trafficked those girls ranked much higher if you're prioritizing a hit list."

"Maybe the others were too hard to get? Or maybe whoever did this is planning to work their way up the proverbial food chain? I don't have any idea where this thing may lead." Cavanaugh tapped a notepad rhythmically against his thigh. "So no one comes to mind?"

"Nobody fits the bill."

Jones stood silently contemplating the implication of Cavanaugh's line of questioning.

"There is another piece to this. And what I'm about to tell you now stays within the confines of this room," Cavanaugh said. "Too early to let it out."

"Understood."

Jones watched as Cavanaugh walked over to Pentlow's corpse, still bound to the bed. The large latex gloved hand of the football-star-turned-detective withdrew a pen from his breast pocket and he bent low, hovering over the face of the dead man. Jones heard a minor cracking sound as Cavanaugh used the pen to pry Pentlow's mouth open. The dead man's jaw creaked like a rusty hinge. Cavanaugh moved back and gestured with his head for Jones to come closer.

"If this is one of you Homicide guys' idea of a sick joke, I'm not interested."

"Just look," Cavanaugh said.

Cavanaugh stepped out of the way and Jones moved closer, looking in to the now-open mouth. Taking a small flashlight from his pocket, Jones illuminated Pentlow's oral cavity. Something glimmered from within, bouncing the light back at him. Jones squinted hard to make out the object.

"Is that a coin?" Jones asked.

"Yup. A nickel to be exact."

"I don't understand."

"Our doer left a calling card," Cavanaugh said.

"You're thinking this might be a serial case?" Jones asked.

"Tokens aren't common and so I'm leaning in that direction. That's a game changer for us in Homicide. Don't get too many of those. I already put a call into the Bureau. They've got an impressive database. If this guy's done it before, they might be able to shed some light."

"You start by asking me if I think a cop could be the doer and you top it with the fact that it could be a serial murder. When you put that together you've got a really bad headline. *Serial Killer Cop* will be every reporter's wet dream," Jones said as he stood erect, distancing himself from the dead man.

"I'm not saying it's a cop. I just want my initial theories flushed out before someone from the Bureau arrives."

"Was he tortured?" Jones asked.

"It doesn't look that way. Autopsy will give us more, but it looks like he was bound and then shot once in the forehead at close range."

"Why a nickel?" Jones asked.

"It's not just any nickel. It's a Buffalo Nickel," a female's voice said loudly from the doorway.

Jones almost jumped at the introduction of the loud comment to their whispered conversation.

Both he and Cavanaugh spun in unison like two oversized ballerinas to address the new arrival. Jones blinked twice, shocked to see an attractive redhead in her mid-to-late thirties standing at the threshold of the room.

"And you are?" Cavanaugh asked.

"Agent Cheryl Simmons, FBI."

"Wow that was quick. I didn't expect them to send someone out. I figured maybe a returned phone call or follow-up email," Cavanaugh said.

"Well this is *my* case. I was in town visiting a friend when my supervisor called me." She looked past Jones and Cavanaugh at the supine body of Pentlow. "I guess it's safe to say that my mini-vacation to Austin has been cut short."

"Wait. Did you just say this was *your* case? I haven't even finished processing the scene," Cavanaugh said taking a step in the direction of the female agent.

Jones watched as Cavanaugh's jovial demeanor shifted and the big man folded his arms in quiet protest. Jones also noticed the smaller framed Simmons didn't seem the least bit intimidated. If anything, it looked like she enjoyed the challenge. Her lip line began to crack into a smile.

"Pump your brakes big boy. I'm the best thing that could've walked into your life. This case would sit unsolved on your desk for years."

"I'm not so sure about that. I've got a solid track record and my solvability rating is higher than most," Cavanaugh said.

"Listen I'm not here to get into a pissing contest with you on this. I've been working the Ferryman case for almost four years."

"Ferryman?" Cavanaugh asked.

"His signature is the nickel in the mouth. Let me guess—was this guy homeless?" Simmons asked.

"Not that I know of. Why?"

"Strange," Simmons responded running her index finger along the lower line of her lip. "I'm stepping in to check out *my* scene."

Jones noticed that the agent never answered Cavanaugh's question. She moved around the room and then stopped at the mirror.

"My boss has already placed the call to your lieutenant," Simmons said dismissively.

"Don't go touching anything. This ain't your scene as far as I'm concerned. I'm going to step out and make a call," Cavanaugh said as he brushed past Simmons in the small space. "Jones, keep an eye on our visitor."

Jones stood awkwardly next to the dead man. He threw his hands up in mock surrender and smiled. "I'm just a visitor."

"Homicide?" Simmons asked.

Jones shook his head. "Sex Crimes."

"Why'd you get the call?"

"The dead guy was involved in a case I worked a short while back," Jones said.

"And?"

"And now he's dead, so I guess they figured I might be able to point them in the right direction."

"Can you?"

"I don't think so," Jones said.

"I'm going to need a full list of people that worked that case with you," Simmons said.

"Okay. Might I ask why?" Jones asked looking out toward the open door of the room where Cavanaugh was red-faced and deeply involved in an intense phone conversation.

"I've been hunting this guy for years. I'm good at what I do, and I've never been able to close the gap."

"So you're thinking that because this killer is one step ahead of you, he's one of us?"

"It's definitely on the table as a very short list of possibilities."

Jones stared at the woman in a light-turquois button-down shirt and navy-blue slacks. The green hue of her shirt accentuated the fiery red of her shoulder-length hair. She moved deeper into the room and closer to Jones. A hint of cinnamon wafted as she closed the gap. The smell was a welcome distraction to the stink of death.

"Well it's all yours," Cavanaugh boomed reentering the room, exasperated.

"I thought you'd see it my way," Simmons said with a cocky smile.

"I've been told to assist you in any way that I can."

"Since your team has already begun processing the scene, it doesn't make sense for me to waste time calling in our techs. Finish up and send me the full case file. If you'd be so kind as to attend the autopsy for me and forward that as well?"

"So, you pretty much want me and my team to do all the grunt work while you take all the credit?" Cavanaugh asked through gritted teeth.

The others in the room stopped their work, pausing to watch the feud unfolding between the two. It looked like a rematch of David and Goliath, and just like the epic biblical battle, the smaller statured combatant was victorious.

"To put it bluntly, that grunt work you're referring to would be a complete waste of my time, but it needs to be done. I work on seeing the bigger picture. If you feel that you're not up to that task, then I will happily make arrangements to have someone else assigned."

Jones looked on as Cavanaugh's cheeks flushed. If this were a cartoon, a kettle would whistle and steam would explode from his ears.

Cavanaugh exhaled long and slow. "I'll take care of it. No worries."

With a momentary truce achieved, everyone in the room returned to their tasks, and Jones looked for his opportunity to slip out. He edged by Simmons and made his way toward his towering friend.

"Who's Nick?" Simmons asked, looking at the mirror.

Jones turned to face the redheaded agent, whose back was to him as she stared at the bloody message. "I'm guessing it's Nick Lawrence."

"Is he out of your office?" Simmons asked.

"Nope. He's out of yours."

"Mine? Nick's with the Bureau?"

"I thought you guys all knew each other," Jones teased.

"Do you have a number for him?"

Jones scribbled Nick's contact info on the back of a crinkled business card that he pulled from his overstuffed wallet and handed it to the agent.

"Thanks. I'll be reaching out to him. Best if you don't give him any advance notice. Understood?" Simmons said eyeing him intently.

Jones nodded and turned to leave. He shook hands with Cavanaugh and mouthed *good luck* punctuated with an exaggerated roll of his eyes.

He left the room containing the departed Pentlow. A light breeze swept across the second-floor landing of the Stagecoach Inn that temporarily muted the odor. Jones had been around death enough to know its stink was now interwoven deep into the fibers of his clothes where they'd linger for the remainder of the day.

Chapter 6

His head violently banged against the plastic surface of the airplane's window, alerting Nick that he'd reached his final destination. A de-icing issue in Austin had delayed his departure, and with each passing minute he'd worried that his opportunity to be by Izzy's side had slipped by. He took out his cell phone as did the other two men crammed into his row. The message to Declan was brief. *Landed. See you in a few.*

Nick shuffled out with the drove of wayward passengers whose bodies, like his, were adjusting to the release from the confines of the past few hours. At a little over six feet tall, Nick never thought of himself as a large man until seated in the cramped space of an airplane. It seemed as though in the last few years airlines had taken away all of the comforts, in particular, leg room. Meals had been replaced by snacks and any additional space had been filled with more seats, making the once luxurious method of travel one of mere convenience.

Exiting onto the sidewalk outside the baggage claim area, Nick scanned the row of cars in the pickup area. Stretching, he inhaled deeply, taking in the dampness of the Connecticut air as a long-term parking shuttle roared by, leaving him in a wake of diesel fumes. He coughed, choking on the acrid taste. Across the way he saw Declan standing outside a black SUV. No smile on his friend's face tonight. He crossed the walkway, and the two men shared a quick embrace followed by a hearty slap on the back.

"It's good to see you, brother," Declan said. "But I hate that it's under these circumstances."

"What's the status?" Nick asked, concern for Izzy permeating the air.

"She's in ICU and they aren't allowing visitors. Her surgery is scheduled for early tomorrow morning. Val's at the hospital now and will call if something changes."

"What'd the doctors say?"

"Not much so far. They err on the side of caution these days. An overly litigious society has left most doctors tight lipped about giving any early prognosis. Rest assured she's in good hands. The docs at Yale New Haven are some of the best in the country," Declan said.

Nick sat in silence taking in the gravity of the situation as the two made their way south on I-91 from Bradley International Airport. He pulled out his cell phone to let Anaya know he'd landed and to check on her trip to Michigan. He looked at his watch and realized she was still in the air and would be for a little while longer. Nick slipped it back into his pocket and stared out the window. A light, but continuous, icy drizzle fell and a thin layer glazed the windshield as the wipers struggled in vain with their task.

"Miss this beautiful weather?" Declan said.

Nick laughed. "Not for a minute."

"You're not going to believe how big the girls are getting. Sprouting like weeds, but crazy as ever," Declan said.

"Last time we talked you mentioned that Laney started a half-day pre-K program. How's she adjusting?"

"The staff is amazing. I was nervous they wouldn't be able to accommodate her needs, but that's been quelled. She's starting to become more vocal and the meltdowns are less frequent," Declan said smiling.

"That's good stuff. I hope that when my time comes to be a father that I can do half as well as you."

Declan laughed. "Is the commitment-phobic Nick Lawrence thinking about settling down? My God, what has Anaya done to you?"

Nick felt conflicted at hearing Anaya's name while rushing to see Izzy. The unresolved feelings bubbled up inside him.

"We've got a good thing going. Let's see where it takes us," Nick said dismissively.

"I'd better be invited if there's a wedding." Declan stopped and gave Nick a wary glance.

Nick felt his cheeks warm and knew that he'd reddened. He was angry at his body's betrayal.

"Wait a minute." Declan cocked his eyebrow. "Has there already been a wedding? Did you guys elope?"

"What? No."

"Well, something's definitely different."

"I don't know what you're talking about," Nick said.

"I can't quite place it, but something's off."

"Can you keep a secret?" Nick asked, already knowing the answer.

Declan's response came in the form a big shit-eating grin.

Nick turned and faced his friend, pausing for added effect. "I'm going to be a dad."

"That's the best news I've heard in a long time. How far along?"

"Eight weeks." Nick exhaled loudly. "Anaya told me this morning."

Declan shook his head. "Wow! You've been on an emotional roller coaster of a day."

"She's going to kill me. I promised I would wait until we made it through the first trimester."

Declan's laughter erupted. "You didn't even make it to through the first few hours."

Nick started laughing and for a brief moment forgot where they were headed.

"Val's going to be so excited. She loves babies. You know that you've just made my life a living hell," Declan said.

"Why's that?"

"Because now she's going to want another one. She's going to catch baby fever." Declan's face softened into a smile. "But I guess it's a win for me. The trying is the best part anyway."

New Haven 30 Miles prominently displayed on the green highway sign ended the levity of their conversation. The two men slipped back into silence. The only sound was the rhythmic scraping of the wipers as they cut their path across the icy windshield.

Although relatively short in distance, the remaining miles of the journey seemed to pass slowly. The anticipation of seeing Izzy in her current situation added a burdensome mental load. Nick followed Declan into the main lobby of the building. The all-too-familiar medicinal smell filled his nose and sickened his stomach. He'd been around it too often in his life and never under good circumstances. *Maybe the birth of his child would change that?*

Val was standing at a small rectangular table set against the wall with her back to them as they entered the waiting room. She methodically churned a thin plastic stir stick into the steaming cup of coffee in her hand. The flat gray of the evening's transition to darkness seeped into the room and blended with the soft glow cast from the ceiling lights. A wave of stress-induced exhaustion swept over Nick and an involuntary yawn caught him by surprise.

Val spun at the sound. The tension in her shoulders dropped at the sight of Declan. Nick hoped that he'd have that same effect on Anaya as their years together passed.

"Hey babe," Declan said moving his hands to her slender hips.

Nick watched as the two shared a quick embrace.

"Oh Nick. Come here," Val said, opening her arms and gesturing him in for a hug.

Nick accepted the invitation.

"It's good to see you again. I'm sorry it took something like this for me to get back this way," Nick said as they separated.

He eyed the coffee pot and slipped past Val, grabbing a cup for himself.

"Any word?" Declan asked.

"Nothing new," Val said.

"Well, I'll take no news as good news at this point," Nick said, taking a sip.

"We should probably head back to our place in a little bit. It's late and they're not allowing visitors tonight," Val said.

"I'm staying. I'd never forgive myself if I wasn't here and—" Nick stopped short, fearing that if he spoke the words they'd become a dark reality.

"If you're staying, then we're staying too," Declan said.

Val nodded her agreement. Nick admired how she gave her support without a moment's hesitation.

"Are you guys sure? What about the girls?" Nick asked.

"Not to worry. My sister's up from Georgia. She doesn't get to see them often and loves any opportunity to be Super Aunt. She's going to be excited to have more time to spoil them," Val said.

"These couches don't look too bad," Nick said. He pressed on the worn vinyl coating of the chair for added effect.

Declan chuckled. "We've slept on worse, much worse."

Chapter 7

Nick lay on the formed cushioning of the love seat with his legs bent and hanging over the wooden armrest. A young redheaded, freckle-faced orderly had brought them a few thin blankets during the course of the night. Nick's jacket was folded into a makeshift pillow and provided minimal relief to his contorted position.

He was awake, and had been for over an hour, but fought against his desire to move. He wanted to let his friends sleep and feared if he got up, the noise from the cushion's release would rouse them. Val was slumped against Declan, their heads merged into one, forming a lover's version of the yin and yang. Nick's eyes traced the lines of the watercolor painting that hung on the wall nearest him. He'd been staring at it since he woke. A sailboat in rough seas with an approaching storm cloud. Nick contemplated his friend's circumstance and felt the picture had captured it perfectly.

The morning light had pushed its way across the reflective surface of the waiting room floor. Val stirred, lifting her head out of the tight notch of Declan's neck, which in turn caused him to blink awake. Satisfied his friends were now up, he rose and shuffled to the refreshment table. Nick poured a cup of coffee from the pot that had been quietly refreshed a little over an hour ago by the same kid that had brought them the blankets. Val wandered toward the bathroom and gave Nick a tired wave as she passed.

"How'd you sleep?" Declan asked, pulling up alongside him at the table.

"Like I fell out of a helicopter and landed on a pile of rocks," Nick said, rubbing his lower back for added effect.

Declan gave a hearty laugh. "It's all that soft living you did in the Rangers."

"Without Rangers, who would SEALs have to look up to?" Nick fired back with a smile and mock uppercut to his friend's ribcage.

Val returned a few minutes later drying her face with a paper towel as she approached. "Did anyone come out yet to give us an update?"

Nick looked at his watch. "Not yet."

As if on cue, the door to the surgical wing of the ICU popped open, and a man in a white lab coat entered, presumably a doctor. He approached the trio cautiously. Nick watched the man's movements and noted the almost imperceptible hesitation in each step the doctor took. A panic alarm rang out inside of Nick's head as loud as church bells on a Sunday morning.

"I'm Doctor Robshaw. Is anyone here family of Ms. Martinez?"

"We all are. Not by blood but closer than most," Val said. "Her mother is making arrangements to fly in from Arizona and should be arriving later today."

Nick watched as the doctor's lips pursed and his brow furrowed.

"What is it?" Nick asked.

"Your friend put up a hell of a fight," the doctor said.

Nick's heart sank as he watched the doctor fumble with the words and avoiding eye contact with the trio.

"Cut to the chase doc," Declan blurted.

"It was a complicated set of surgeries. I don't know how much you all know about the nature of her injuries?"

"Is it her back? How bad are we talking?" Declan asked.

"The damage to her spine was severe, but our biggest concern became the brain bleed. It was a high-risk procedure, but wholly necessary."

"Jesus," Nick hissed.

"The impact of the crash ruptured blood vessels in her brain. The damage was extensive. We tried to relieve the pressure. I'm sorry." The doctor paused and momentarily broke eye contact with the group. "We've got an amazing team in that operating room. Some of the best in the country, but the intracranial bleeding was devastating. She succumbed to her injuries."

Nick felt the eyes of Val and Declan wash over him. The impact of the doctor's words coupled with his friends' stares caused his head to spin. The room began to whirl and the features of the people around him blurred. His face flushed, and Nick couldn't decide if he were going to vomit or scream. He chose neither, standing there numb with shock.

"Doctor?" Val asked as if she'd misheard the explanation.

"She didn't make it," the doctor said. "I'm very sorry for your loss."

Nick's hands slid down the outside of his jeans toward his knees. The next thing he knew he was on all fours staring at his hazy reflection cast back at him from the linoleum floor of the waiting room.

Val's hair brushed his cheek, and he felt her hand calmly rubbing circles in the center of his back. She was speaking softly but the words were barely registering. He breathed deeply, trying hard to right himself.

"Let's get you up into that chair," Val said.

Nick suddenly felt a strong hand that he assumed to be Declan's grip him under his arm. With their assistance he found the rigid cushion of the love seat he'd been a prisoner of for the past several hours. He looked up at his friends who returned his inquisitive gaze with a look of compassion and concern.

Embarrassed by his collapse, Nick hung his head. "I'm sorry. I don't know what came over me."

"Don't apologize to us," Declan said. "Not now. Not ever."

Nick looked back up at his friend. The former SEAL's normally rugged exterior was somewhat softened, and Nick saw the wetness of fresh tears still matted in Declan's eyelashes. This caused him to crumple again. A whimper escaped as he fought, without success, to suppress his pain.

The three sat silently consoling one another for what seemed like an eternity. The doctor had retreated into the recesses of the restricted area marked *Medical Personnel Only*, leaving them in the privacy of the waiting area to grieve the death of their friend.

"We should be here to soften the blow when her mother arrives. Not something you tell someone over the phone," Val whispered to Declan.

"I can't believe she's gone. There were so many things I never told her." Nick's voice cracked, and he stopped himself from finishing his train of thought.

The doors to the surgical area re-opened behind them and the same doctor reappeared, stopping abruptly after passing through its threshold.

"Who's Nick?" Doctor Robshaw asked.

Nick, bookended by Val and Declan, turned slightly in the uncomfortable chair to face the doctor.

"I am," Nick said. "Why?"

"When we initially brought Isabella into the ER we looked through her phone trying to locate an emergency contact number of a family member," Doctor Robshaw said.

"Izzy," Nick interrupted.

"Excuse me?" the doctor asked.

"Izzy. She hated being called Isabella," Nick said.

"Sorry. When *Izzy* came to us, we went through her cell phone. We found her mother's number, but there was an unfinished and unsent text message to you, Nick," Doctor Robshaw said.

In his haze Nick hadn't noticed that the doctor was holding a cellphone in his left hand. Nick swallowed hard at the sight of it.

"Would you like to read it?" the doctor asked.

Nick didn't speak, terrified at what throaty noise might erupt from him if he did. He only managed the slightest nod of his head.

The exchange made, the doctor left again, back behind the boundary of the secured doors.

Nick held the phone with two hands. The unknown gravity of the message contained therein gave the small device an incomprehensible weight. He forced himself to breath.

"Do you want us to give you some privacy?" Val asked softly.

Nick shook his head, knowing he needed the strength of his friends to get through this. He flicked his finger across the shattered screen, opening it. He tapped the messenger app and it opened. His name was positioned on top of the list of messages. The word *draft* in red italics noted the unfinished text. He sighed loudly and tapped lightly on the conversation.

He read silently the words never sent, never spoken: *Nick I really wish that things had turned out differently between us. I've started this message a thousand times before but never finished it. I don't know why, but I woke up this morning thinking about you. I am going to say this not expecting that you'll respond but I need to say it. I lo"*

The cursor blinked next to the "o" as if taunting him. The message unfinished and unsent hit Nick hard. Those words they'd never said to each other, but he knew were always tucked just beneath the surface.

Nick gave way to its weight, letting the phone slip out of his hand and onto the floor.

No one moved. His friends sat frozen.

"I killed her," Nick mumbled.

"What are you talking about?" Declan said.

"She was trying to reach me. Message me. She was distracted. It's my fault," Nick rambled almost incoherently.

"That's absurd. You can't make this worse than it already is. You had absolutely nothing to do with her death," Declan said.

Nick didn't answer. His eyes stared out at the painting on the wall and envisioned a massive tidal surge smashing the small vessel.

"Take solace in the fact that the last thought she had was of you," Val said.

The words hit Nick like a sledgehammer, and he crumpled into the crux of her neck, sobbing uncontrollably. He let the pain roll down her shoulder in the form of pent-up tears.

Chapter 8

"You're not staying in a hotel! Val won't hear of it." Declan said with a resolute look. "You get the pleasure of sleeping at Casa de Enright. Prepare yourself for a five-star experience."

"I think I'd rather just be alone for a bit," Nick responded. His words dribbled out of his mouth with the fervor of a man with his head on the chopping block.

"It's not up for debate."

Nick noted the resolve in his friend's eyes and slumped in defeated resignation.

"All right Just don't expect much in the way of company," Nick said.

"With you, I never do," Declan said.

Nick appreciated his friend's attempts at humor, but it only managed to sink him deeper. *Life is strange.* A year ago, he'd been looking at Enright for an armed robbery. Fast forward to the present and that same man is his closest friend.

They pulled up to the two-story gray colonial. It looked much as it did the first time Nick had been to the house, minus the burning minivan with Declan's wife and daughter trapped inside. He and Izzy had saved them from a fiery death that day. Now she was dead.

Declan's large Chevy Suburban barely fit on the small driveway. The wheels on the driver's side settled a few inches onto a swath of lawn, more dirt than grass from the repeated abuse of the heavy automobile. The branches of the ice-covered maple tree hung low, hovering a fraction of an inch above the roof. Nick saw the inconsequential garage that wouldn't comfortably fit a go-cart, let alone a car, and understood why the Enrights crammed both family vehicles into the minimal square footage of the cracked asphalt driveway. Declan had left just enough space for Val to squeeze the Corolla in when she arrived home.

Nick stepped out and slipped on a slick spot of black ice invisibly coating the ground. He grabbed the door to keep from falling.

Declan saw Nick's near spill. "Sorry. It's pretty slippery. I haven't had a chance to throw some salt down yet."

"No worries. I plan on leaving a negative review on Hotels.com," Nick said.

The thought of mocking his friend's humble abode carried an immediate shot of guilt, knowing the financial battle Declan's family was facing with the cost associated in raising their autistic youngest daughter Laney. He knew Declan well enough that his friend wouldn't be offended, but it felt wrong and he assumed the oversensitivity was due to the current circumstance.

"The girls will be home from school soon. They'll be excited to see you. I'm still not sure what we're going to tell them. They loved Izzy too," Declan said.

"I'll leave that to you. The parenting thing isn't my strong suit."

"Not yet, but it will be sooner than you know," Declan said smiling.

Nick followed Declan to the side door of the house, gingerly stepping with caution as he traveled over the skating rink of a walkway. The air was raw, and Nick quickly realized that his tolerance for it had been zapped by his time in Texas. He shivered. He began vigorously rubbing his arms in an attempt to remove the cold's grip as he entered the tight space of the Enright family's kitchen.

"Gotta kick the shoes, buddy," Declan said. He started taking his off on the threshold carpet before entering further into the house. "I've been domesticated."

"Anaya has the same rule. I guess like wild stallions, all men can be broken." Nick chuckled softly. "It's a good rule if you think about it. Especially considering the nasty places our job typically sends us. Nobody should track those remnants into our homes."

Declan nodded absently as he set about placing his shoes into a boot caddy and hung his coat on a peg near the door. The Enrights made good use of their minimal square footage. With two adults and three children, you had to be a master of consolidation when living in a two-bedroom, one-bathroom home.

"Do you want anything to eat or drink?" Declan asked.

"Is it too early for a beer?" Nick asked.

"Hmm, let me consult the wisdom of my spiritual advisor, Jimmy Buffet." Declan closed his eyes and put his index fingers on his temples as if he was in deep meditation. "We're good! It's never too early. Coors Light okay?"

Nick watched as Declan retrieved two cans from the fridge. He was happy to see that his friend would also be partaking in an early afternoon beverage. At least he wouldn't be drinking alone.

Val and Declan had taken separate cars to the hospital. Nick had heard the crunch of the tires when she pulled into the driveway shortly after their arrival, but she'd remained outside. Nick now understood what she'd been doing as Val dropped a bag of rock salt near the storm door before entering.

"Excuse me? Drinking during the day?" Val said, eyeing the cans.

Nick looked at her and gave a sheepish grin. Val took the can out of Declan's hand.

Val laughed. "Get your own big boy!" she said taking an exaggerated sip.

All three got a slight reprieve in the levity of the moment.

Nick popped the tab, the loud metallic click followed by the familiar sound of release. He raised his drink, tapping the bottom against Declan's.

"To Izzy," Declan said.

Nick said nothing. He had no words for his dead friend. He took a long pull from the can.

"Heard from Anaya?" Declan asked.

"She's still in the air. I'll talk to her later."

Nick's phone vibrated in his pocket. He pulled it out, briefly looked at the screen, and then tapped the answer icon, bringing the phone to his ear. Nick took a sip of the cold beer and wandered away toward the dining area of the kitchen.

"I really don't want to talk about it now. I just left the hospital and am getting settled. I'll hit you up when I get back in town," Nick said before letting Jones speak.

Nick had received a text message from Jones earlier requesting that he call him ASAP. Nick had responded by telling him that Izzy was dead. It was a blunt message, but he knew that Jones would take no offense. Jones responded that he needed to talk to him about a case. Nick had no interest in discussing the tragedy of a victim's life when he was dealing with his own.

"I'm sorry about Izzy. From the little I knew of her, she seemed like a great person. But that's not why I'm calling. You've got a problem," Jones said.

"What problem? What are you talking about?"

"Remember Richard Pentlow?" Jones asked.

"Yeah. The kiddie diddler from the motel. Why? What'd he do now?" Nick asked.

"He's dead."

"Hmm. Well that means there is one less sicko in the world. What's his death got to do with me?" Nick asked.

"There was a message."

"Jones, stop beating around the bush and tell me what the hell is going on!" Nick exclaimed.

"I'm not supposed to tell you any of this. I was instructed not to, but I didn't want to see you get blindsided. The case has already shifted to your side of the house," Jones added.

"Why did Pentlow's death go federal?"

"It's a serial murder," Jones said.

"So, you're telling me a serial killer offed Pentlow?" Nick asked.

"Yup."

"I still don't get what this has to do with me. You know that I don't work those types of cases," Nick said, pulling deeply from the can in his hand.

"There was a message at the scene. It was addressed to you," Jones said. His tone was serious, and the West Texas twang was suppressed.

Nick was silent.

"It's kind of dark. Maybe it'll mean something to you?" Jones asked.

"Go ahead with it."

"I don't have it memorized, but it was something about prevailing when the justice system fails."

"I thought you said it was to me?" Nick questioned.

"That part I do remember verbatim. It said, *Nick, what stands up tall but reaches low?*"

Nick went silent again.

"Nick? Are you still there?" Jones asked.

"Yeah. It's just been a hell of a day. Who's working the case from the Bureau?"

"An agent by the name of Simmons. She came in and took over from Pete Cavanaugh and his crew from Homicide. She's definitely got some balls."

"Never heard of her," Nick said.

"Well that's about to change. She's going to be looking to talk to you," Jones said.

"I figured as much."

"I didn't want you to be caught with your pants down on this. I've got to run. We'll talk more when you're back this way. And Nick, we never spoke about this," Jones said.

"Understood. I'll be in touch. Thanks for the call," Nick said. He slipped the phone back into his pocket.

Nick turned. Declan, obviously within earshot of the conversation, raised his can and cocked his eyebrow before taking a gulp.

Declan gave a knowing shake of his head. "When it rains, it pours."

"That's the damn truth." Nick said.

Val went upstairs to change out of the clothes she'd slept in.

The side door opened, banging loudly against the nearby cabinet as Abigail and Ripley, Declan and Val's two oldest girls, clamored into the kitchen dropping their backpacks on the floor. They paused for only a second to kick their shoes into a light pink bin on top of a small wooden bench. They rushed past Nick, without taking notice, and barreled into their father. Nick watched contentedly as the two fought to occupy the territory of their father's neck as they wrapped their wiry arms around him.

Declan embraced both girls tightly. The Enright girls had only been away from their father for one night, but to watch the girls' reaction, you'd think it'd been months. Nick looked on with excited anticipation of what his own future held.

"Look who stopped by for a visit, girls," Declan said, redirecting their attention.

"Uncle Nick!" The two girls cheered in unison and charged him.

The maniacal embrace of the children gave Nick a fleeting reprieve from the weight of Izzy's death and a needed distraction from the phone call he'd just received from Jones. In an instant they were gone, disappearing down the hall and up the stairs to what Nick assumed was their bedroom. He could hear their giggles pass through the low ceiling of the house.

"Early dismissal today. Never a dull moment in the Enright house," Declan said.

"I guess I'll be experiencing that first hand soon enough." Nick said this as he thought of Anaya and their unborn child thousands of miles away.

Chapter 9

"I'm sorry I didn't call you back last night. Or this morning. I've been a little out of whack since getting here," Nick said.

"I understand. No need to explain yourself to me. I'm just so sorry I'm not there for you right now," Anaya said.

"You are. Knowing that you're in my life is all I need. How are you settling in? Make sure to say hello to Mouse for me," Nick said.

"What's next? Have arrangements been made yet?" Anaya asked.

"The funeral is being planned by her family. I'm assuming that it will be later this week. Her family is scattered so they're going to want to delay it long enough for everyone to get here."

"Would you like me to come?" Anaya asked timidly.

Nick wasn't sure if he registered a note of hesitancy in Anaya's voice as she asked this.

"No."

Anaya said nothing.

Nick felt that his answer was too abrasive and tried to back pedal an explanation. "I just mean it doesn't make sense for you to disrupt your time with Mouse. What you're doing for her by supporting her as she starts her new life is important. Enough people have failed that girl in the past, and I don't want us to be added to that very long list."

"She looks great! And the home is absolutely amazing."

"That's good to hear. I'm happy for her."

Nick let the tension in his shoulders drop. He'd felt a subtle nervousness during Anaya's trip and was content knowing that she had arrived safely. After his dealing with Khaled, Nick's sense of security had been shattered. He saw firsthand the ease at which attacks could be carried out on the unsuspecting public.

"I'm going to let you go. As soon as I figure out how long I'm going to be staying here, I'll call you."

"I love you Nicholas Lawrence," Anaya said.

"I love you too. Take care of our baby," Nick said.

He hoped that Anaya hadn't picked up on the confliction in his voice. Being back in Connecticut had brought forth a swell of emotions, and the tidal wave of devastation at Izzy's passing had left him drowning in a sea of unanswered questions. He ended the phone call and rejoined Declan and Val in the living room.

"How's she doing?" Val asked.

Nick noticed the subtle innuendo in the question and shot Declan a look. His friend and former Navy SEAL couldn't manage to keep the secret of Anaya's pregnancy for less than an hour.

"Wow, Fort Knox you are not, sir," Nick said, shaking his head.

"Sorry brother, she knows all my secrets," Declan said. He gave Nick a smirk and high fived his wife. "Home team."

"The good, the bad, and everything in between," Val said, reciting her mantra and tapping her can against her husband's.

Nick shook his head and managed a half smile.

"She's good. She arrived safely and is really excited to spend some time with Mouse."

"Anaya's really amazing," Declan said. "Not many people in this world keep promises anymore. She went above and beyond to get Mouse to Michigan. That little girl is lucky to have you two in her life."

Nick's phone buzzed again. He looked down at it and didn't recognize the number, but did recognize the Dallas area code. He dipped back into the kitchen and answered.

"Hello?" Nick asked.

"Is this Nicholas Lawrence?" a woman's voice said.

"Yes. And it's Nick."

"Okay *Nick*. This is Cheryl Simmons. I work out of the Dallas field office. I'm investigating a case and need to speak to you regarding it," Simmons said.

"Okay, go ahead," Nick said. He made a conscious effort not to accidentally betray the information Jones had given him earlier.

"Not over the phone," Simmons said bluntly.

"Well that's going to be a bit of a challenge for me since I'm in Connecticut," Nick said, annoyed.

"I've made arrangements to get you back here. You're going to need to return immediately."

"I'm not going anywhere. I'm here for a friend and agent who died today," Nick responded.

"I know where you are and what you're doing. It's been cleared from the top down. You're coming back, and it's not up for further discussion." Simmons spoke clearly, enunciating every syllable, but with no trace of emotion.

You know and you're still telling me to come back? Nick thought. *Either Simmons is the worst human being on the planet or this case is more complicated than Jones initially indicated.*

"I'll see what I can do," Nick said trying to keep up a level of resistance.

"You're scheduled on a 5:15 p.m. flight out of Bradley. I'll send you the flight information," Simmons said.

Nick looked down at his watch. It was 2:00 p.m.

"Jesus. Thanks for the heads up," Nick said sarcastically. "That's going to be cutting it close."

"Then I'd suggest you hurry up," Simmons said, returning the sardonic tone.

"Question. If you're out of the Dallas office, why are you working an Austin murder?" Nick asked.

"I never said anything about the murder taking place in Austin. Sounds like you've got some friends out this way speaking out of turn," Simmons said.

Shit. He realized she hadn't said anything about the case facts and Nick just exposed himself. Exposed Jones. One thing was for certain, Agent Simmons didn't miss much.

Nick waited for her to pry deeper.

"I'm currently working out of Dallas, but I go wherever a case takes me. I'm BAU." Simmons said this last statement with added affect.

Nick fumbled with a response as Simmons ended the call. He stared at phone and sighed heavily. He hadn't worked much with the Behavioral Assessment Unit since entering the Bureau. He knew that only an extremely small number of agents were selected, and the chosen were held in high regard.

Declan walked in and opened the fridge to retrieve another libation. Nick noticed that one of the top shelves was held together with duct tape. Normally the sight of it would have prompted Nick to make a witty comment, but he was lost in thought.

"Ready for another round?" Declan said. He stood holding up two more cans of the Rocky Mountain classic, the blue of the mountains indicating their coldness.

"I can't. I've got to run. I just got called back to Texas," Nick said.

"I don't understand. Your boss knows why you're here?" Declan questioned.

"It's one of those cases that apparently can't wait."

Nick looked at his watch again out of habit even though he'd just checked it less than a minute before.

"My flight leaves in three hours. Do you think you can shuttle me back to the airport?"

"Val's not going to be happy that you're leaving so soon," Declan said, returning the cans to the packed interior shelf of the fridge.

"I know. Hopefully, I can make it back for the funeral. Although, I'm not a real fan of 'em," Nick said.

"Me neither. I've got more friends in the ground than above these days. Sadly, your ugly ass is one of the few still left standing," Declan said.

Nick chuckled softly. It felt strange to laugh at anything on this day, but the release felt good and he was grateful for his friend's sense of humor.

"It's not for lack of trying, but I guess I'm unkillable." Nick ran a hand over the scar on the left side of his stomach where he'd been impaled by a knife less than a year ago.

"But I guess both of our survivability just went down a bit," Declan said.

"How so?"

"Without Izzy around to save our butts we've got to be more careful. I for one think we should invest in extra body armor, but with our finances I'll probably have to settle for bubble wrap."

Nick knew the truth in Declan's statement. Izzy had come to the rescue for both men more times than he cared to admit. If it hadn't been for her quick thinking, Nick would've been dead long ago. The raised skin of the thick scar tissue that ran down his left arm, above the elbow, was a testament to that day and the tourniquet she'd used to save him.

After saying a quick goodbye to Val and the girls, Nick now sat in the confinement of the passenger seat of Declan's older model red Toyota Corolla. He adjusted the seat back to give some much-needed leg room.

"I can see that you're enjoying the spaciousness of this sweet ride," Declan said laughing.

"It's great. I feel like I've been stuffed into a clown car."

"Sorry buddy, but Val has to pick up Laney from pre-K in a bit, and I feel better when she uses the SUV in this kind of weather," Declan said.

"No need to apologize. And please tell Laney I said hi and that I'm sorry I didn't get a chance to see her."

Nick looked around the small car and felt Declan staring at him. Declan gave a miniscule grin that bent wider as he looked over at his friend.

"What's so funny?" Declan asked.

Nick shrugged his shoulders, broadening into a full smile.

"What?" Declan asked.

"I've never ridden in a getaway car before," Nick said.

Declan sighed and drooped his head in mock shame. "Are you ever going to let me live that down?"

"Probably not," Nick said.

The Corolla headed north on I-91 toward Bradley Airport travelling on the same road that Izzy had been killed on the previous morning. He was on the same path but in the opposite direction. It wasn't lost on him that this was symbolic of their failed attempt at a relationship.

Chapter 10

Sleep hadn't come to him during the return flight to Austin. A long day punctuated by the bounce and skid of the 737 on the cool tarmac of Bergstrom International. The plane's touchdown left Nick suddenly exhausted as the weight of the past two days of heartache crashed down on him, compounded further by the endless hours of travel.

The airport was relatively deserted minus his accompanying travelers. Nick looked down at his watch. The digital numbers read 10:30 p.m. The majority of flights had long since reached their final destinations, and the overnight cleanup crew was already hard at work preparing for the next day. He bypassed baggage claim. His lowly backpack was all that he carried. His suitcase was with Anaya in Pidgeon, Michigan. He'd borrowed a change of clothes from Declan, as they were about the same size, and was wearing a blue sweatshirt with a Rick and Morty logo centered on the front. Declan had given strict warning to take care of his beloved hoodie.

Simmons had sent him a message that she'd be sending someone to pick him up when he arrived. Nick stepped outside onto the curb and scanned for his ride. A young man with a crewcut, who looked no more than twenty, stood by a dark blue sedan and waved to him sheepishly. Nick looked over his shoulder to verify that this gesture was for him and then, seeing nobody behind him, nodded a silent acknowledgement.

"Agent Lawrence?"

"Yup," Nick said as he walked up to man.

"I'm Gary Salazar. I was told to take you directly to see Agent Simmons," Salazar said.

Nick noticed that the young agent's face flushed during his introduction. Salazar awkwardly stuck out his hand. Nick gave it a firm shake.

"When did you graduate?" Nick asked.

"That obvious huh? Last week."

"Jesus, how old are you?" Nick asked.

"Twenty-three."

"Straight out of college to Quantico?"

"Yessir. I'm very excited to get started. It's always been a dream of mine ever since I can remember."

Nick said nothing and entered the vehicle, taking his place in the front passenger seat. He unshouldered his backpack, setting it at his feet.

"It's a real honor to meet you Agent Lawrence. I've heard all about you at the academy. They gave a lecture seminar on how you and your team stopped that terrorist," Salazar gushed. "Really impressive stuff."

"I'm sure most of it was bullshit. And call me Nick."

"Yessir," Salazar said

"Drop the sir. I'm not your supervisor and this isn't the academy." Nick realized that he was more snappy than normal and tried to dial back. "So where are we meeting Simmons?"

"At your office."

The sedan pulled out from the airport and onto the arterial stretch of State Highway 183 that circumvented the congestion of downtown Austin. Although the evening rush had dissipated hours ago, there were still pockets of traffic. The endless sprawl of Austin's population created a commuter nightmare.

The trip was relatively short, just over forty minutes, but after the day of roundtrip traveling Nick was suddenly overcome by fatigue. He fought to keep his eyes open. The low hum of the engine and rumble of the tires worked against his battle against sleep.

His phone startled him as the alert vibrated, acknowledging the receipt of a new text message.

It was Anaya. *How are you holding up?*

Nick had totally neglected to let her know about his return to Texas. He debated on whether he should continue holding back that information and wait until tomorrow.

He thought, *No need to worry her tonight.* He knew her too well and came to the conclusion she'd be more upset that he'd kept it from her. She'd read more into it than necessary.

He responded. *I'm in Austin. Just landed. Called back for a case. I'll tell you more about it when I call in the morning.*

Be safe. Love you, she responded.

Get some rest. Love you too. Nick slipped his phone back into his pocket and then rubbed his eyes. He was glad that she didn't press him further on the matter. He had to prepare himself to meet Simmons.

"Got any coffee going back at the office?" Nick asked, breaking the silence of the drive. He hoped that conversation would help with the drowsiness.

"Not sure. If not, I can make some," Salazar said.

His eagerness to please would have been endearing if Nick wasn't so depleted. He had little room for pleasantries at the moment and eagerly awaited an end to this night. Nick looked out the window, recognizing the familiar landscape of the buildings set against the night sky and knew they'd be arriving at their destination shortly.

"Tell me about Simmons," Nick said, staring into the night without looking over at Salazar.

"Not sure what you want me to tell. I only just met her today. I'm still in the orientation phase and have no cases yet so I got tasked to pick you up from the airport. Low man on the totem pole."

"Well aren't you fresh out the gate from recruit land? Didn't you have to do assessments back at Quantico, or has that important piece of investigations been torn from the lesson books?" Nick asked.

"Yeah, but that was just training. I've never tried to do it outside of the academy. Not sure I'm the best guy to ask."

"Give it your best shot. I've never met Simmons. So here's your test. Take a minute and give me your behavioral assessment of her. After I meet with her, I'll give you your first *real world* grade," Nick said, cocking his eyebrow and looking down his nose at him for added effect.

"Okay. This isn't some kind of prank you play on the new guy is it?" Salazar said.

"I hope you're not this hesitant when it comes to field work," Nick said, knowing this would nudge the eager-to-please young agent.

"Well here goes nothing. She's small statured, in her early to mid-forties. She works out. Probably some combination of cardio work with some Pilates or strength training. She's got red hair that appears to be natural and she—"

"I hope to God you're not going to tell me you think she uses conditioner. Give me the assessment. You're telling me what she looks like. I want you to tell me about *her*," Nick chided.

"You sure this isn't going to get back to her?" Salazar asked self-consciously.

"Are you going to fail your first test as an agent? We're pulling up to the building in less than a minute. Tick tock."

"She overcompensates with aggression. I would describe her as hostile. She's very direct and seems to derive pleasure in making people uncomfortable. Simmons is obviously intelligent, otherwise she wouldn't be in the position she's in. There's a certain clout about her, and the other agents, including the boss, give her wide berth when she moves about the office. I know she is BAU so maybe she's spent so much time studying other people she forgot how to be one herself. Basically, if I had to sum her up in one word it'd be bitch."

Salazar pulled into a parking spot in the nearly vacant lot of the FBI's Austin field office. Technically, it was referred to as a satellite office or resident agency of the bigger San Antonio field office, but Nick didn't care about such labels. Salazar put the vehicle in park, but left the engine idling.

Nick gave a wide-eyed look toward the rookie agent in the driver's seat as if he'd been offended at the assessment.

"Do you know that Simmons is my long-time partner and best friend?" Nick said.

Salazar's head fell forward and came to rest on the worn rubber of the steering wheel. "Shit. I should've known better."

Nick watched the tormented Salazar squirm in anguish. He allowed this to continue a moment longer before deciding to let him off the hook.

Nick chuckled at his ruse. "I'm just messing with you. Like I said, I've never met the woman. Wow, you almost fell apart on me there. I thought I was going to have to call in the medics," Nick said, giving the green agent a slight smile.

Salazar exhaled loudly. "You definitely got me good. I'm not going to lie; I wasn't going to go back in that building if that were true. The woman terrifies me."

"Well let's go meet this scary lady," Nick said, exiting the vehicle.

He shouldered his backpack and marched off toward the building.

He entered through the first set of doors which automatically opened as he stepped on a sensor pad. That same sensor pad also calculated his weight and stored it in a database. Three different cameras affixed at different heights and angles captured both agents as they stood in the entrance. Nick then entered the sequence code into the keypad that allowed after-hours access to the building.

The interior doors slid open, and Nick stepped into the all-to-familiar main lobby with Salazar in tow. Nick considered this building a second home. A home now host to a fiery redhead with an agenda unknown to him. His concern grew with each step he took.

Chapter 11

The elevator chimed, alerting their arrival on the third floor. The doors parted, and Nick was greeted with the glow of the pale lighting of the office space. It seemed brighter than normal in contrast to the dark, moonless night.

"Just so you know, she's kind of taken over here," Salazar said meekly.

"Great," Nick said, letting out a sigh.

He walked toward his cubicle, among the small cluster of partitioned work spaces. He caught movement out of the corner of his eye and saw the woman who'd ordered him back to Texas without any care for the tragedy that befell Izzy. She stood hunched over the conference table sifting through a stack of files. She must've heard their entry because she turned her head. Her distinctive shoulder-length red hair fell to the side as she visually assessed him. Salazar's physical description had been spot on and she was actually more attractive than he'd anticipated, but the sight of her caused him to involuntarily clench his teeth.

She gestured to an empty chair to her left but didn't smile. Nick didn't acknowledge her and passed by, proceeding directly to his desk. He dropped his backpack at the foot of his three-drawer filing cabinet, grabbed his mug, and then made a beeline for the small break room.

He smelled the coffee as he entered and saw that a full pot waited. So far it was the only upside to his forced return. He poured the steaming black liquid into his cup. A hint of hazelnut wafted up. Nick wasn't particular about his coffee as long as it was piping hot and fully loaded with caffeine. He tossed a scoop of sugar in and gave it a quick swirl. Nick held the cup close to his lips before taking a sip allowing the steam to lick at his face.

He turned to see Salazar standing in the doorway. Nick gave a half-hearted smile.

"If you're all set, I'm going to head out," Salazar said, glancing over his shoulder toward Simmons. "Unless you want me to stay."

"I think I can handle myself. I'll grab one of the spare cars to get home," Nick said.

"It was really great meeting you. I can't wait to tell my buddies from the academy that I met the legend."

"You can also tell them that the stories are always far different from the reality." Nick paused, taking another sip. "It's time for me to see how accurate your assessment of Simmons was. If you were half-right, then I'm in for a long night."

Nick noticed that Salazar wasted no time in vacating the office area. Nick turned his sights on the conference room. A glass panel lined the wall, exposing the rectangular room with a large oval table at its center. There were several television monitors attached to the walls bookending the table. The back wall was an end-to-end dry erase board for writing notes. The room was used for big cases that required the brain power of multiple investigators. It looked like Simmons had taken it upon herself to effectively occupy that territory.

Even though the door to the room was open, Nick knocked lightly on the glass, announcing his presence, although he knew she was well aware of him.

"Have a seat. I see you helped yourself to the coffee I made," Simmons said.

"Long day," Nick responded flatly.

"It's going to be a little bit longer."

"Listen Cheryl, I came here at your request on a really shitty day. So, let's get right to it," Nick said.

He took a pull from his mug trying without much success to swallow down his anger.

"I'm sorry for your loss, but this situation is time critical."

Nick looked at the woman before him. She remained standing and was stacking the files she'd been pouring over when he'd arrived. Simmons was attractive, and now that he saw her up close, he noticed that her eyes were a bright emerald green that complimented her fair skin and fire red hair. He now understood why Salazar had difficulty evaluating her personality. Nick worked hard to see past her physical beauty and begin his own assessment.

"Why was I pulled from a family emergency? Why am I here?" Nick asked.

"I'll get to that, but first I'm going to need to ask you to answer some questions," Simmons said.

Simmons cleared off the table space nearest them and sat down. She reached down to a worn leather satchel resting against the leg of her chair and retrieved a small audio recorder and pad of paper.

"What's with the recorder?" Nick asked, eyeing Simmons.

"I like to make sure that I get everything correct. I can't have any of the details slip past me. I have the notepad but I prefer to observe more than write when I talk to someone."

"Talk or interrogate?"

"Talk. Unless you feel an interrogation is warranted?" Simmons said. Nick noticed that she was giving him an intense stare.

"I'd hope not. I still don't even know what I'm doing here," Nick said.

"I think you know more than you're letting on. And from our earlier phone conversation it looks like somebody gave you a little heads-up."

"Apparently not enough for me to understand what any of this has to do with me," Nick said.

"That's what we're going to try to figure out," Simmons said, reaching her hand out toward the recorder. "I'm going to press record now. Understood?"

Nick nodded. He wasn't used to being on this side of an interview and he didn't like it.

"Tell me about Richard Pentlow," Simmons said.

"Pentlow? He's a child rapist."

"And?" Simmons asked.

"When he was caught he was found in a hotel room with an eleven-year-old girl tied to a bed."

"What happened to him?" Simmons asked patiently.

"He was arrested and was awaiting trial. Last time I saw him he was in the Travis County Jail. We had a long talk and he confessed," Nick said.

"And what did the little birdie say when he called you?"

"I know Pentlow's dead," Nick said curtly.

"You know more than that Agent Lawrence," Simmons said cocking her head to the side exposing the gentle contour of her neckline.

Nick sat silently. He leaned back and folded his arms, emotionally closing himself off.

"I hope we're not going to play games for too much longer. But no worries either way because I can go all night," Simmons said.

The double entendre was not lost on Nick.

"There was a message," Nick said.

"And?"

"And, that's it. I don't know what the message said. Only that it was written to me," Nick said, trying to salvage the slip up and protect Jones.

"Okay. Now was that so hard?" Simmons said, softening slightly.

"I didn't kill Pentlow if that's what you're driving at," Nick said.

"Did I ask you if you killed Pentlow?" Simmons said.

Nick said nothing.

"You don't fit the bill anyway," Simmons said.

"What do you mean?"

"I've been tracking the Ferryman for years. I'd like to think I've got a particular knack for seeing the details. You don't fit the profile I've developed," Simmons said.

"How so?" Nick said, trying to subtly seize control of the interview from Simmons.

"For starters, you're too big. The Ferryman is small in stature," Simmons said. "And your psych doesn't match."

"My psych profile?"

"That's way too big a box to unload tonight," Simmons said.

Nick couldn't tell from her flat facial expression if she'd just tried to make a joke.

"You keep referring to this guy as the Ferryman. Why?" Nick asked.

"The killer leaves a coin in the mouth of his victims. It is a symbolic gesture."

"Symbolic of what?"

"A reference to the boatman, Charon, from Greek mythology, who ferried the dead across the river Styx. The coin is his calling card or token," Simmons said.

"And I'm involved in this how?"

"He wrote a message to *you!*" Simmons said bluntly.

"What did it say?" Nick asked.

"I was waiting for you to ask me that question." She paused and pulled an 8x10 glossy out of the file folder closest to her. She pushed the picture across the shellac finish of the table toward Nick. "Take a look for yourself."

Nick unfolded his arms and reached over, pulling the photograph the remainder of the way over to him. He picked it up and took a second to study the image.

"Is this written in blood?" Nick asked.

"Pentlow's."

Nick said nothing and squinted hard, reading the message again. *Where the system fails I prevail. Nick, what stands up tall but reaches low?*

"Any thoughts on why he's naming you in his message?" Simmons asked.

"Not a clue. You?" Nick said, laying the photo back on the table between them.

Now it was Simmons who sat silently.

"I'm guessing the doer, the Ferryman, knew Pentlow was released on bail. Maybe even posted it. I'd start there," Nick said.

"It's being looked into."

Simmons reached across the table and plucked the photograph from the table, returning it to the brown leather of her satchel.

"And we'll get into the details of the case at a later date. Right now I want you to focus your thoughts on why the Ferryman would name you in the message," she said.

"Like I said, I've got no idea."

"The Ferryman seems to have some sense of connection with you. Whether it's real or imagined, we'll have to find out," Simmons said.

Nick allowed the thought to marinate and he didn't like the taste it left. Catching the interest of a serial killer couldn't have much of an upside.

"Why me?" Nick asked more to himself.

"Whatever the reason, it's not good," Simmons said.

"No shit."

"Get some rest. I'll be in touch," Simmons said.

Nick watched as she stood and turned her attention back to her boxes. She began shuffling a pile of files into a frayed cardboard box on the floor. A wave of anger flooded him.

"That's it!? You're done!? You flew me back for a fifteen-minute conversation that we could've had over the phone? You are some special breed of asshole!" Nick spat the words.

"I don't do phone interviews," Simmons replied.

The lack of emotion in her response only fueled his fire. Nick sat seething in a barely controlled rage.

"You don't do phone interviews? That's the best answer you've got? I guess you don't give a shit about my former partner who died on the table today? She was one of us. Ten times the agent you are!"

"I'm doing my job. I don't allow anything to get in the way of that."

"Well, that's crystal freakin' clear. I hope you don't have a family because I'm sure you wouldn't put them before your godforsaken cases!" Nick said in a low growl. He immediately realized the hypocriticalness of his comment, but anger stopped him from making any attempt to refute it.

Simmons's eyes narrowed, darkening the brightness of the green. Nick realized he'd struck a nerve and was satisfied by his effective deliver of the blow.

"Have a good night," Simmons said curtly.

The glimmer of anger that had enveloped Simmons seemed to recede as quickly as it had come, like a passing storm cloud.

Nick stood up. His six-foot frame towered over Simmons. His fists clenched and released in sync with the pulsing of his increased heart rate. He gritted his teeth, grinding hard and sending a ripple along his jawline. Simmons stopped organizing the files and faced Nick.

"Is there something else? If not, I'd tuck that weak attempt at intimidation back wherever you found it," Simmons said contemptuously.

Simmons seemed to be unaffected by Nick's rage. He thought, at some level, it actually appeared she was enjoying it. He noticed the corner of her lip begin to bend upward into a hint of a smile.

Nick exited the conference room without saying another word. He moved quickly to his desk, the vortex that trailed him tossed papers from a nearby desk. Without looking back, he grabbed his backpack and keys to the government-issued VW Jetta and made for the elevator.

As the doors were closing he heard Simmons call out to him. "I wouldn't go too far Agent Lawrence!"

Nick slumped against the cool metal wall of the elevator. His eyes felt heavy and seemed to droop at the same rate as the descending elevator car. He exhaled slowly and took stock of the past two days. At its start, he'd learned he was going to be a dad. The joy of that moment had been stolen from him by Izzy's tragedy. Her death was still incomprehensible, and he pushed away the thought of it. And now he was the target of a serial murderer.

A killer had taken interest in him. It wasn't the first time, but the last almost cost him his life. Nick rubbed his left side. The impression of the wide raised scar could be felt beneath the thickness of Declan's sweatshirt. It served as a constant reminder of that terrifying night. Sleep had not come easy before, and now it rarely came at all. This new threat would undoubtedly add to his perpetual insomnia.

The wind whipped hard as he stepped out into the cold of the Texas night. He sat in the Jetta and looked up at the building he'd just left. The third floor was still lit. Agent Simmons would apparently be burning the midnight oil. As much as he hated her right now, he realized that under a different set of circumstances he'd have appreciated her tenacity.

Chapter 12

What bends but does not break? What weeps but does not cry?

A whistle sounds as the air coils around the fast-moving branch cutting through the thick warmth of the southern night. The sound is an early warning of its impending arrival. Then comes the pain, a sensation like that of being burned and cut at the same time. Each strike is more painful than its predecessor as old scars are reopened, marking deep the history of this violence. No sounds emanate from the inflicted. No satisfaction will be given to the vicious blows. No begging for it to stop, punishment will not be his reward. It ends as abruptly as it started.

Then the whispers follow, weighted heavy with the scent of sour of whiskey and cheap aftershave, "I'm sorry. It's for your own good. I'll make you better. I promise."

The memory fades, but will resurface again, as it always does on these nights.

The cold air would keep most people indoors tonight. But there are those who don't have places to go, some by choice and some by circumstance. These creatures scurry about in search of scraps, feeding off the discards of others. Human cockroaches digging through trash and sleeping in alleyways. Most pass by without seeing them, intentionally erasing their existence from view. It's easier that way.

It's always tough to make the selection. There are so many to choose from, but tonight's had been one of design rather than random opportunity. In the soft yellow of the street light's glow a man appeared from behind a dumpster. The cold apparently had no effect on him because he was only clothed in a white tank top tie-dyed in a swirl of stains. The vagrant completed his ensemble by wearing black basketball shorts accented by his white socks pulled up high, cresting the bony knees.

The man ran his dirty hands through his greasy hair, painting the gray with grime like a poor man's version of Just For Men Touch of Gray. The long hair and unkempt beard would've been considered a grayish white, but the lack of hygiene had given it a yellow-brown tint. He protectively cradled the contents of a brown paper bag. The cylindrical shape denoted his drink of choice for the night was some variety of canned beer. Mostly likely a 40-ounce of malted liquor, ensuring the most bang for his hard-earned buck.

Watching someone who doesn't know they're being watched is always fascinating. A person's truest self is exposed during those moments when they think they're alone. *What if someone were watching me? What would they see?*

The bearded man walked on toward an alleyway that was poorly lit. He paused only briefly to warm himself on the steam spewing up from a sewer grate. Then he disappeared back into the shadowy recesses of the narrow space between the closed shops.

Following someone who doesn't know they're being followed is a thrill in and of itself. Following the bearded man was more of a challenge because of the deserted street. Movement can be masked in a crowd, but much more difficult absent of such. It's essential to move quickly once committed. With speed comes noise and therefore it has to be tempered with external conditions. The wind proved to be an ally and its wild gusts masked each pursuing step. The light of the street no longer captured the bearded man's silhouette as the Ferryman slipped into the pitch blackness of the alley.

The vagrant was balancing on his tip toes hunched over an open dumpster, examining the object of his treasure hunt. The Ferryman stood directly behind the unaware man, absorbing the seemingly timelessness that existed before the chaos. His left hand rubbed the coin, a reminder of purpose.

Less than a foot away the knife slipped silently out from the tightly strapped, worn marbled leather of the sheath. The force of the first blow buried the blade deep between the cockroach's lower ribs and drove upward until the hilt's contact with the man's flesh stopped the momentum.

The Ferryman anticipated the man's reaction as he grabbed at the first wound. The blade had already been torn free and the whistling wheeze indicated the lung's puncture, reducing the stabbed man's scream to a raspy hiss.

The bearded man spun to face his attacker, his eyes widened in terror. The Ferryman seized this opportunity. The second thrust of the blade struck hard into the man's neck. Horror gave way to shock, his legs buckled, and he collapsed to the ground.

Watching someone as they take their last breath is unlike anything else. So unique that most people have never experienced the twisted magic wherein life transitions into death. The beauty is that each person accepts death differently. The Ferryman watched as the man died, absorbing the elixir of the last seconds of anguish. The Ferryman inhaled deeply, imaging he was taking in the dead man's essence. Soul eating.

The man on the ground twitched, his right hand clawed hard into the cracked concrete of the alley floor, and then all movement faded away. His yellowed beard was now dark with his blood. The gloved hand of the Ferryman spread open the dry, cracked lips of the dead man and placed the coin under his tongue.

The ritual complete, the Ferryman walked back into the light.

I am good. I am better. Without me they'd be lost. I carry them away.

I am the Ferryman.

Chapter 13

Nick sat at his kitchen table. He looked at the clock. It read 7:30 a.m. Rubbing his eyes, he tried to get a fresh perspective on yesterday's events. The clock clicked, taunting him with each passing second. He picked up his phone to call Anaya. She was an early riser too, and he wanted to make sure that she'd settled in.

He'd never worried about her before, but with a baby on the way he was suddenly filled with a constant sense of worry. Izzy's death was a tragic reminder of how life can change in the blink of an eye.

A knock at the door disrupted his train of thought. He grabbed his pistol from the counter near the sink and bootlegged it behind his back. He didn't think a serial killer would come knocking, but at this point in his life he didn't know what to expect. He peered through the peephole.

He would've been as surprised to see the killer as he was to see Cheryl Simmons standing on his stoop looking around nervously. She stood holding a recycled gray cardboard tray containing two Starbucks cups.

Nick stuffed the Glock into the rear waistline of his jeans and opened the door, hugging himself against the cold that was as unwelcome as his visitor.

"Before you say a damn thing, I want you to know that what I did last night was the right thing. I needed to see you face to face. I needed to see your answers to those very simple questions," Simmons said.

"Did I not answer them to your liking? Why are you here?" Nick said, making no attempt to hide his annoyance.

"I've been here all night."

"You've been here all night? What the hell is wrong with you?" Nick asked.

"I had to be sure."

"Be sure of what?" Nick asked.

"That it wasn't you," Simmons said.

"I waited as long as I could before waking you. By the looks of it I could've come earlier,"

Simmons said shivering subtly. "Are you going to let me in?"

Nick didn't respond.

"Listen, I brought coffee as a peace offering."

Nick reached out and accepted the cup, whose warmth could be felt through the corrugated cardboard sleeve. He tipped the cup in her direction, giving an indication of the possibility of a truce, and stepped back from the threshold allowing her to enter.

"What do you mean you had to be sure it wasn't me?" Nick asked.

"I've had a theory for a long time now that Ferryman is in our line of work. A cop, agent, someone who knows how we operate. Someone who can manipulate the system."

"And you thought that someone was me?"

"It would've been a pretty smart move for the killer to name himself in a message. It would derail most investigators," Simmons said.

"Then why are you brining me coffee?"

"Because it's not you," Simmons said bluntly before taking a sip from her cup.

"How do you know that?"

"The Ferryman claimed another victim last night. And because I sat outside your apartment and know that you never left."

Nick walked into the kitchen and dumped two heaping scoops of sugar into his cup, pondering what she'd said.

"Why not just let me stay in Connecticut? If there was another murder while I was away, then it would've given you the answer without dragging me across the country and away from people who need me," Nick said. The embers of last night's interrogation started to burn again, and he fought to quell his urge to yell.

"I thought about it, but there is another reason I brought you back."

"I can't wait to hear," Nick said sarcastically.

"The Ferryman has picked you. Taken an interest in you. If you weren't the killer, then I figured maybe I could use it to my advantage."

"So, what now? I'm now your bait?" Nick asked.

"Looks that way to me," Simmons replied.

Nick said nothing and took the opportunity to gulp the sugary liquid, letting it burn its way down.

"It's only happened one time before," Simmons said.

Nick noted the seriousness in her tone. "And who was that lucky person?"

"Me."

"Shit."

"It started with a simple message, and then it got personal," Simmons said.

"Personal how?" Nick said.

"He came after my family," Simmons said, breaking eye contact.

"Jesus. What happened?" Nick asked, concern ebbing from his words.

"My parents. The sick bastard killed my parents." Simmons's eyes watered as she spoke, causing them to shimmer more brightly.

Nick noticed that without the false bravado and pit-bull attitude, Simmons was stunning. The subtle humanity evident in her reaction at mention of the death of her parents instantly changed his opinion of her. He didn't pity her but could empathize. And from that understanding, Nick realized that he had a new-found respect for Cheryl Simmons.

"Well, your forcefulness with regard to this case makes a hell of a lot more sense to me now," Nick said.

"I've been close before, but then poof. Nothing. Completely off the grid until now," Simmons said.

"Why now? And why me?" Nick asked.

"Wish I knew. That's the million-dollar question."

"What's next?"

"I'm glad you asked… partner," Simmons said, giving a half-cocked smile.

"Partner?"

"You and I are gonna be besties!" Simmons said, flicking her hair with feigned enthusiasm.

"I've got a ton of case work. I can't just up and leave my victims hanging while I run off to chase a ghost."

"You're officially reassigned."

"Reassigned? I don't work murders, especially not serial cases," Nick pleaded.

"Not that much different than sex crimes except for the bodies."

"If this guy targeted your family, what's to say he won't come after mine?" Nick asked.

Simmons dipped her head and broke eye contact with Nick.

"I agree, it's a real problem. We need to get a protective detail assigned to your closest family members," Simmons said seriously.

"My girlfriend is in Michigan. She just got there yesterday. I should fly out to be with her, so I can keep her safe," Nick said. His mind raced to find acceptable solutions.

"Not sure that's a wise move. If the Ferryman's sights are on you, it's not going to matter where you go. At least here, we can throw more assets at the problem. Best bet is to get her back here as soon as possible. In the meantime, I can coordinate with the Detroit field office to get a security detail to post on her up until then. Any other family close?"

"My mother. She's at Pine Woods. It's a retirement community not too far from here. She's in a ward designed to handle late-stage Alzheimer's."

"That shouldn't be a problem. Most of those facilities are relatively secure. We can probably get local support for that. Anyone else?" Simmons asked.

"That's it. My father and brother are deceased."

"Sorry to hear that."

Nick didn't like to talk about that part of his life. Patrick's suicide had left a hole that time had failed to heal. Izzy had been the only one he'd confided in. That was, of course, until Anaya came along.

"I've got to call Anaya," Nick said, grabbing his cellphone off the table. "She's got to know what we're up against."

"I'll give you some privacy. When you're done meet me in the car."

"Okay," Nick said.

"We've got a crime scene to work. *Partner,*" Simmons said, closing the door behind her.

Chapter 14

"Here she comes," Cavanaugh said.

"The sexy redhead?" Ed Spangler asked, looking up from a squatting position.

"Trust me, once she speaks you'll see there's nothing sexy about that woman at all."

"We'll see about that," Spangler said.

Nick followed behind Simmons as she entered the alleyway, crossing under the yellow Police - Do Not Cross tape. Any time Nick moved past the onlookers and onto a scene, he couldn't help feeling that it was like being a VIP to the macabre. Or, as he had bluntly put it many times before, *the front row seats to the freak show.*

A short potbellied man with a high forehead and glasses stood up. He removed his purple latex gloves and tossed them into an open bucket marked Disposal. He adjusted himself, tucking his unkempt shirttail into his wrinkled khakis. He reached his hand out to Simmons. She accepted it, and the stout man shook it vigorously.

"Ed Spangler, Crime Scene. The big guy here says you're running the show," Spangler said, breaking the handshake and thumbing back at Cavanaugh.

Nick looked on as Spangler barely took notice of him. Cheryl definitely caused a distraction to the team working the scene. Spangler looked starstruck. He was surprised the ogling wasn't followed by howling catcalls and whistling.

"Ed, nice to meet you face to face. I didn't get a chance to see you at the motel. But I did see the report you drafted and your summation of the scene. Solid work," Simmons said.

It was as if Heidi Klum had leaned in and given him a kiss. Spangler's face flushed at the compliment.

"Cavanaugh, you said she was a real bitch. She's seems really nice to me," Ed said over his shoulder to the enormous, now mortified, Homicide detective.

"What? I never—. Ed you son of a—," Cavanaugh stammered.

"No. He's right. I can come off as a real b-i-t-c-h. Isn't that right?" Simmons said looking at Nick.

Nick gave an exaggerated nod emphasized with a wide roll of his eyes. "You have no idea."

"Meet my new partner, Nick Lawrence," Simmons said.

"We know Nick. He's been basically slumming with us city guys off and on for years. We told him he's too ugly to be in the Bureau," Cavanaugh chided.

"Someone's got to keep you guys in line," Nick jested.

"What's Jones going to say when he hears that you're cheating on his large brisket-loving ass for a redhead?" Cavanaugh boomed.

Nick gave a wide smile.

"Well, now that all that's out of the way, what've we got?" Simmons asked.

"This fella here had a bad night of dumpster diving," Spangler said. "It looks like a couple of alley cats got the best of him."

Nick gave a tired smile at the weak joke. He was sure Spangler had used some variant of it on every new face arriving at the scene.

"Two puncture wounds. One lower right ribcage. The second, left side of the neck. The neck wound was the fatal one. Early guesswork would be middle of the night. Hard to tell until the M.E. gets him on the table," Cavanaugh said.

"So, we are assuming knife? Any reason to think otherwise?" Simmons asked.

"It'd be my guess. The size of the wounds would be consistent with that," Spangler said.

Simmons walked closer and gave a quick once over, looking down on the dead man. She turned back toward the group.

"Let my partner see the token," Simmons said.

Nick gloved up, putting two gloves over each hand. His big hands tested the limits of the latex's elasticity, indicated by the faded white stretched across the ridges of his knuckles.

"We've already done photos, and everything's been tagged for collection. Just watch your step," Spangler said.

"It's in the mouth," Cavanaugh said.

Nick took up the same position Spangler had been in when they first arrived. He squatted down next to the head of the dead man. The bearded jaw was already open. Nick balanced his forearms on his knees and leaned in, hovering close to the man's mouth.

He peered closely. Amidst the sea of rotten teeth, he saw the circular metal shape buried underneath the corpse's twisted tongue. Nick stood and the rush of blood in his legs caused him to wobble.

Nick looked at Simmons who was staring at him intently. The potential that this killer was coming for him, for his family, shook him to the core. He blew out the tension with a loud exhale.

"Two bodies in less than a week. It's never happened this quickly before. I've never seen the deaths timed so close together," Simmons said.

"What do you think it means?" Nick asked solemnly.

"I don't know. Maybe he's mad or really trying hard to get your attention." Simmons turned toward the street.

"Well, he's got it now," Nick said, looking back down at the body of the homeless man.

"One thing I do know is that we better get our asses in gear and find this guy before the next body drops," Simmons said.

Nick stripped off the gloves and tossed them into the bucket. Even in the cold of the morning, his hands were now slick with sweat.

"Don't worry boys, the bitch is leaving." Simmons cast a glance at the large detective. "Cavanaugh, I'll be checking in later."

Nick tried to shrug off the awkward departure, giving Cavanagh and Spangler a half-hearted shrug of his shoulders as he hustled after Simmons.

Chapter 15

"I understand why you're here, but can you make yourself a little less visible?" Anaya asked, leaning into the window of the unmarked Michigan State Police vehicle.

"I'll do the best I can, but I've got orders to maintain eyes on you and the house at all times. Rules are rules," the trooper replied.

"I know. It's just the little girl over there has been through a lot, and I want to minimize any unnecessary judgement from neighbors. She's trying to start a new life here."

Anaya looked back at Mouse who sat on the stoop of the front door petting her golden lab. She couldn't help but be amazed at the child's resilience. The trauma she'd faced would've crippled most people, but Mouse was not most people. Anaya's goal was to make sure that she got a chance at normalcy, a chance for her to be a child. Seeing her now gave her hope that this was becoming a reality.

The trooper grunted his reluctance but caved to Anaya's request. "I'll move down the street a bit. I guess there isn't really another approach to the house except by boat, so it should be all right."

"Thank you. It will only be a few more days until I leave. I really appreciate you looking out for us," Anaya said.

She turned and began walking up the white stone driveway of Mouse's new home. The house was set back from the road and nestled against the expansive ice-covered Lake Huron. From certain angles, when looking out from inside the spacious open layout of the house, it appeared to be floating on the water. Anaya smiled broadly, pleased with herself for getting Mouse to this destination. It couldn't have been a better location to begin life anew. She thought of how Nick almost gave his life making sure this little girl would have a chance. She loved that man without reservation. She knew that he'd put as much into raising his own child who was growing inside her.

Her contentment was interrupted by the muffled chime of her phone penetrating the thick lining of her heavy winter coat pocket.

"Speak of the devil, I was just thinking of you," Anaya said.

"I can't stop thinking about you."

"We're okay. Promise," Anaya said.

"It's killing me that you are so far away, but I agree that it's for the best right now. I'm wrapped up in this case, and I wouldn't be able to protect you the way I should," Nick said.

"I can handle myself, remember?"

"I know, I know. It's just... um... different now," Nick said.

"We're going to be fine. The protection detail is here. You focus on finding this guy and let me worry about everything else," Anaya said.

"Hey is Mouse around? I want to say hello," Nick asked.

"Sure is. Hold on," Anaya said, handing the phone off.

"Hi Nick!" Mouse said.

"Hey tough girl, I'm really sorry I couldn't be there to see you," Nick said.

"No worries. I understand," Mouse said.

"What are you and Anaya going to do today?"

"Not sure. I think we are going to make some hot cocoa and take a walk out on the ice.

We'll send you a pic," Mouse said, speaking a mile-a-minute.

"So glad you're loving it out there. Anaya said you've got a dog?"

"Yup."

"That dog couldn't be in better hands," Nick said happily.

"I named her Izzy," Mouse said.

Nick's throat constricted, and he paused to clear it. Izzy's name coming out of Mouse rocked him.

"She saved me," Mouse said in a whisper.

"Me too. More times than I can count and, in more ways, than I can say," Nick said.

Nick wiped the moisture from his eye. "She'd have loved to know that you named your new best friend after her."

"I'm so sorry about what happened, Nick," Mouse said.

"You know better than most the crappy hand that life deals us sometimes." Nick rubbed his temple and tried to clear his mind. "You enjoy your time with Anaya. Keep an eye on her for me."

"Okay. I'll see you next time," Mouse said.

"You bet. Next time for sure."

Nick pocketed the phone and looked over at Simmons who was intently focused on the wet roadway. Not cold enough for ice, but cold enough to make it a miserably slow commute back to headquarters.

"How's she holding up with all of this?" Simmons asked without taking her eyes off the road.

"She's good. The security detail is on site. Thank you for setting that up," Nick said.

"No problem. I'm surprised they were so quick to respond to my request."

"What's the plan now?" Nick asked.

"I've got to bring you up to speed on this investigation, and fast." Simmons adjusted the wiper setting to deal with the varying rate of precipitation and continued, "Are you up for this?"

"I've never backed down from a fight before and don't plan on this being the first time."

"Good to know."

Nick stared intently ahead.

"You just seemed a little off after the phone call," Simmons said, shooting him a glance.

"Just a lot to process, I guess," Nick said.

"Is Mouse your daughter?"

"Mouse? No. Would be proud if she was. Tough as they come. Anaya and I helped her out of a really bad spot not too long ago. She was just adopted by her foster family in Michigan," Nick said, allowing his pride to shine through.

"I didn't mean to pry. I just overheard the nickname and assumed."

"No need to explain. How about you? Kids?" Nick asked.

Simmons sighed and fidgeted in her seat. "Not for me. Life dealt me some bad cards in that department."

"Sorry," Nick said.

"Not your fault, right?" Simmons gripped the wheel tighter, exposing the white of her knuckles. "Any plans of starting a family of your own?"

"Plans seem to have had nothing to do with it," Nick said.

His cheeks flushed at his subtle admission. He watched to see if Simmons picked up on it.

"So that explains it then," Simmons said.

"What?"

"Why this Ferryman threat has you so messed up. How far along is she?"

"Two months," Nick said.

"Well look at you. You're going to be a father. Excited?"

"I just found out the day before yesterday." Nick said.

"You had a hell of a start to your week," Simmons said.

"That's the understatement of the century."

Nick stared out at the red chain of brake lights that danced across the windshield as the wipers worked to clear the drizzle. The zigzagged towers of Austin's downtown skyline were dimed by the storm clouds overhead. The Ferryman was out there somewhere, and Nick needed to find him in the worst kind of way.

Chapter 16

The office was warm. The thermostat, set too high in an attempt to offset the cold of the day, left the office ten degrees warmer than necessary. Nick shed his heavy coat and rolled up his sleeves. Simmons made a direct line to the conference room and seemed unaffected by the drastic change in temperature. Nick felt the eyes of his coworkers as he followed behind the redhead. He forced himself not to engage their looks. He'd aligned himself with Simmons and didn't want to betray the fragile trust they'd just recently established. Nick knew this alliance provided him with the best chance of catching the Ferryman.

Nick shut the door after he entered the conference room, closing them off from the others. Without Simmons on the attack, the room had returned to its comfortable standing. He tossed his wet coat on a nearby chair and sat. It took only a second before Nick realized that he was again sitting in the same chair as the night before. Simmons must've noticed this too, because she grinned widely as she placed the large cardboard file box on the table between them.

"Don't worry. No more interrogations from me," Simmons said.

"Good to know. I don't think I'd last another round," Nick snarked.

"I'm going to need you up and running on these cases, past and present. An extra set of eyes never hurts. And I've heard you have a knack for investigations."

"Thanks. And I agree whole-heartedly that it's always good to have someone else look at things from a fresh perspective," Nick said.

"To be honest I don't usually work with a partner." She nibbled at her bottom lip. "I've found that I'm better off on my own."

"Many hands make light work," Nick said.

"Not for me. It's more of a burden."

"Then why ask me?"

"It's simple really." Simmons stopped unpacking the box and paused, with a file folder in hand. "Bait."

"Bait? There's that word again. I hope that I can be more assistance to you than a piece of cheese in a trap."

"I hope so too, but if not, at least I can tie you to a chair and see if the bad guy comes. Figuratively, of course," Simmons said with a wink.

"Geesh, that sounds bad."

"Bad for you, but good for me."

"I'm not sure I like the sound of this." Nick stared hard into the intense green of Simmons's eyes.

"Not sure you have much of a choice. Look at it this way, for whatever reason the Ferryman's picked you. He's coming sooner or later. And I'd rather use that and try to control it. If we can draw him out, then it would give me an advantage that I've never had."

"So, you want me to keep to my routine? Not draw any suspicion that we're concerned so he feels comfortable making a move?"

"See! I knew you were a smart guy. I just want him to move without worry. Maybe he'll get sloppy and make a mistake."

"You keep saying him. How do you know the Ferryman is in fact a man?" Nick asked.

"Most serials are. The percentages of females are so low, it's typically not entertained in most initial theories. Even at the Behavioral Analysis Unit, we tend to jump to that conclusion. We try not to, but time-tested data says these types of predators are most commonly male. Similar to the percentage of the pedophiles you hunt. Although there are always exceptions," Simmons said pensively as she tapped a pen on the desk. "I'm impressed that you caught that. Let's entertain your question. What makes you think the Ferryman is or might be a woman?"

"I don't. I just said it's a possibility. I haven't been working the case, and you've obviously developed your profile. I didn't mean to question it," Nick said.

"That's irrelevant to my question. Why do *you* think it's a possibility?"

"The stab wounds on the latest victim," Nick answered.

"Go on."

Well, the first one I'd assume was the rib shot. And I'd guess the dead guy to be about 5'10" to 6 feet tall. Basically, he's average to slightly above average in height. If the killer was standing, that knife would've come in from low to high."

"A tall man could make that wound by driving upward like this." Simmons took the pen in her hand and held it pointing up with her thumb as the guide. She then made an upward arcing motion.

"True, but I think the second wound is more telling," Nick continued.

"How so?" Simmons asked.

"I'm assuming that the stab wound to the neck was the second attack. So it was done at an upward angle."

"How'd you deduce that about the neck wound?" Simmons said.

"The cut was not straight across, as it would've been if the doer were of similar height. So, based on that, I'm thinking it also came from low to high," Nick said, studying Simmons's reaction to his conjecture. Her face was stoic and didn't betray any indication of her opinion.

"You got all that from being on that scene for such a short time?"

"Look, murder isn't my forte. I could be way off," Nick said.

Simmons took up the tapping of her pen again. "Well, I guess what they say about you is true."

"And what's that?" Nick asked putting his guard up slightly in preparation for her answer.

"That you've got a gift for this kind of work. More than I'd thought you would. I did my checking and most of the praise comes from your skills as an interviewer, but it appears you've got a great eye and can apply it to a scene as well."

"Thanks. Did I get it right?" Nick asked, accepting the compliment without much gushing or fanfare.

"We'll have to wait until I hear from Cavanaugh or Spangler, but I concur with your initial thinking to some degree."

"What am I missing?" Nick asked.

"I've spent the better part of four years developing the Ferryman's profile. Early on I looked hard at the possibility of a woman due to the height factor and some other indicators. I worked up a full list of potential physical and psychological aspects."

"And what made you change your mind?" Nick asked, sensing there was a *but* coming.

"*He* attacked me."

"Attacked you?" Nick asked wide-eyed.

"I told you I was targeted when I first began my investigation. I got a similar message to yours. I told you he killed my parents. What I didn't tell you was that he tried to kill me too."

Nick watched Simmons break eye contact. Her pale skin became almost translucent and she immediately redirected her energy, busying herself separating out the files in front of her into different stacks based on the date of attack.

"Wait, you're telling me you went head to head with this madman?"

"Not something I like to talk about."

"Tough. You're going to talk about it to me. I need to know everything there is about this guy."

"Let's just say my profile was wrong and it almost cost me my life," Simmons said, lifting up her shirt just enough to expose her left side, above the hipline. She absently ran her index finger across the three inches of jagged ridges of white scar tissue.

Nick nodded at the gesture. "What was it?"

"Knife."

"Looks like we could be twins," Nick said, allowing a slight grin to form. He yanked up his shirt, revealing a similar marking. His still had a red discoloration to the puffy scar left by the dead man that had given it to him.

Simmons smiled and the color in her cheeks returned to normal.

"I took one in the gut a little while back," Nick clarified.

"Seems like we've got more in common than I previously thought," Simmons said.

"You said your profile was wrong? How so?" Nick asked.

"I was correct about the Ferryman's stature. He was just slightly taller than me. I'd put him at about 5'5" with a wiry frame. My workup had the Ferryman pegged as a female. I had a lead and was looking hard at a stripper at one of the clubs in downtown Dallas."

"A stripper?" Nick asked.

"Yeah. It seemed a good fit. She'd been brutally assaulted by a homeless man a few years prior. Beyond that, she came from a broken home. And when I say broken, I mean it was demolished. She had a history of abuse that would make a prisoner of war cringe."

"So, what happened?" Nick asked, totally engrossed.

"I was doing surveillance on her club, trying to learn her patterns and see where she went after work. I was set up about a block down the street." Simmons paused, and her breathing became more rapid. "A guy in a hoodie walked by my car and flicked something through my open window. At first I thought it was just an asshole trying to be funny, until I picked it up."

"What was it?"

"A nickel," Simmons said.

"A nickel? Like the ones he leaves behind?"

"Exactly. A Buffalo nickel with the Indian head carved out to look like a skull with Medusa-like snakes for hair. His calling card. The death token he marks his victims with. At this point, I'd collected enough from several victims to recognize it immediately."

"I don't mean to interrupt, but what the hell's a Buffalo nickel?" Nick asked.

"It used to be a fairly common practice to deface a coin. The Buffalo nickel was popular because of the design. The large Native American profile on one side and the buffalo on the other gave artists a larger platform to manipulate than other coins. People used to engrave and modify the coin."

"I'm not tracking. So why does he use it? It must hold some significance," Nick said, confused.

"It's known by another name. These altered coins are commonly referred to as a hobo nickel."

Simmons paused and opened a thick case file. She fished out a photograph which was tightly focused on one of these coins. Nick examined the picture closely. The face of the coin had been converted into a skull. The blood of some unsuspecting victim was painted onto the etched surface.

"So, the connection is what? What am I missing?" Nick asked laying the photo on the table. The vacant eyes of the skull taunted him.

"Don't worry, I didn't see it at first either. He primarily targets the homeless. Thus, the sick bastard's sense of humor using the hobo nickel as his tribute."

"All the victims have been homeless?" Nick asked.

"Yes, for the most part but with some exceptions. A lot of conjecture has been made as to why," Simmons said.

"Pentlow wasn't homeless," Nick interjected.

"Not by our definition, but after you arrested him, his wife left him and moved out of state. His house was foreclosed on. So, technically he *was* homeless. But like I said, he does make some exceptions. Like in the case of my parents."

"Okay. Sorry I didn't mean to cut you off. I'd just been meaning to ask you about the coin," Nick said.

"No worries. It's a lot to take in."

"Back to that night, what happened when you realized he'd tossed the coin into your car?" Nick asked.

"I gave chase, of course. The little bastard was quick. He tore off through a nearby warehouse. I called it in to my partner who was set up on the other side of the nightclub."

Nick listened as Simmons recounted the incident. As she relived the intensity of that night, her cheeks flushed, the color complimenting the red of her hair.

"He completely caught me off guard when I entered the warehouse. It was fast. Really fast. He must've been waiting for me behind the door because he grabbed my ponytail as I ran into the room. I can still remember that pain. I thought he'd snapped my neck."

Simmons absentmindedly rubbed the back of her neck as she recalled the moment.

"I thought he punched me in the ribs. It took me a minute to realize I'd been stabbed."

"I can say with genuine assuredness that I completely understand what you mean," Nick added.

"I was able to grab his knife hand while the knife was still inside. I fought hard to keep him from using it on me again. At some point during the tussle, he struck me hard in the side of my head in the temple area. Just before I lost consciousness, I managed to pull down the bandana that masked his face."

"So that's how you know it was a man?"

"All I saw was the scruff of a beard. So, either the Ferryman is a man or the bearded lady," Simmons said, adding some levity to offset the intensity of the retelling.

"Any other details about his appearance?"

"He wore these red tinted sunglasses. It's all I remember before I blacked out," Simmons said softly.

"How come he didn't kill you?"

"I ask myself that every day. I'm guessing my partner must've spooked him."

"He didn't see anything?" Nick asked.

"Nothing."

Both were silent.

"Crazy, right? How quickly life can turn on a dime, or our case, a nickel," Simmons said.

"You couldn't be more right about that," Nick said.

He thought of Izzy and how many times she'd been there for him during those times of turmoil. Life had thrown him a massive curveball, and now he needed to figure out what the world would be like without her. Although their personal relationship had stalled out, just knowing that she was out there somehow always made him feel safe.

Izzy wouldn't be there to save his ass this time. Nick didn't like the thought and he involuntarily shuddered, shaking it off.

Chapter 17

"Mr. Lawrence?"

"Yes," Nick answered into his cell phone.

"It's Doctor Whitmore over here at Pine Woods. I know that you are out of town on vacation, but I need you to come here right away," the doctor said.

Nick heard the tension in the physician's voice and it concerned him greatly. "I'm back. My trip was cut short. What is it, Doc?"

"Your mother passed away," Whitmore said.

"What?" Nick said, suddenly unsteady.

Nick looked down at his watch. He'd lost all track of time. It was almost 9:15 p.m. He'd left Simmons back at the office a few hours before, after taking a stack of files home with him. He was trying to get up to speed on years of investigative efforts in a matter of hours.

He'd been absorbed in case file after case file, devouring the information like a pig after the pour of a slop bucket. Time slipped away while he sat on the worn leather-backed chair in his quaint study. An office space that would soon most likely be converted into a baby room. His mind was racing, and all of these thoughts came crashing down on him haphazardly, making it impossible to comprehend the doctor's words.

He heard the sound of the doctor's voice but understood none of what was being said.

"What? I—don't—I mean how—when?" Nick babbled.

"I'd rather discuss this with you in person. When can I expect you?" Whitmore asked calmly.

Nick snapped into focus and was already moving through the condo grabbing his jacket and keys.

"I'm on the way and will be there shortly."

"I'll be here to greet you when you arrive," Whitmore said.

Nick ended the call, dropped his phone into his pocket, and dashed madly out the door into the brisk night air. He barely registered the icy wind that pelted against his face. The only thought on his mind was his mother and how he'd failed to be there at the end.

Nick made fast work of the distance between his house and his mother's assisted living facility, weaving the Jetta in and out of the minimal suburban traffic.

The doctor had delivered the initial blow, but he had a hard time accepting it. Even though he knew deep down that he was already too late, he still felt an undeniable compunction to get there quickly. A self-preserving thought resonated that if he got there fast enough he could reverse things or prove the doctor wrong. It was irrational thinking and even though he was aware of its lunacy, he continued his maniacal trek.

Nick continued his reckless operation of the small German four-door as he accelerated into the parking area of Pine Woods Retirement Center, slamming on the brakes and skidding to a stop in front of the main entrance.

Nick left the car running and ran to the entrance. The automated sliding doors opened too slowly, and Nick pried at them, forcing the mechanics to work at his desperate speed. He rushed into the main lobby and was greeted by the familiar face of Doctor Whitmore.

"Mr. Lawrence, I'm so sorry for your loss."

"I still don't understand. She was fine the other day. I stopped in to see her before I left on my trip," Nick said through ragged breaths.

"She was. We're still running some tests and I'll hopefully have more for you once I have those results, but prelims are indicating heart failure. You know that she's been in a weakened state for quite some time now," Whitmore said.

"Why would you let me go on vacation? Why would you tell me that she'd be in good hands?" Nick's anger seeped through gritted teeth.

"Mr. Lawrence, there would've been nothing you could have done even if you were here. I understand you're upset. Please, take a moment to calm down before we go to see your mother. Would you like some water?"

Nick said nothing. He took long slow breaths trying to regain his composure. The doctor stood by patiently waiting and didn't interrupt. It was obvious to Nick that the man was comfortable with death and people's adverse reaction to it. Nick was too, but not when it came to family. His spiraled mood was compounded by the thought of his mother dying alone at Pine Woods. And the image of it made him sick.

"Can I see her?" Nick asked. His voice had returned to its homeostasis.

"Of course. When I realized you were in town I had staff leave her. We wanted to wait for you. If it provides any consolation, your mother looks at peace."

The doctor turned and proceeded to walk into the restricted wing of the facility reserved for residents who required additional care. Nick's mother's dementia had dictated the move to this section of the hospital months ago.

He followed one step behind the doctor. Although Nick towered a good six inches taller than Whitmore, he couldn't seem to keep pace with the man's stride. It was as if Nick's shoes were encased in concrete, each step harder than its predecessor.

The doctor broke the silence. "At least she had one visitor today."

"What do you mean visitor?" Nick asked.

"An attorney. He wanted to verify the conditions of your mother's room."

"Verify the conditions? You're not making any sense."

"It's okay Mr. Lawrence. I take no offense in you ensuring your mother's receiving the best treatment," Whitmore said.

Nick stopped dead in his tracks and the doctor in turn did the same, turning to face him.

"I didn't send an attorney," Nick said.

"I don't understand?"

"I said I didn't send an attorney. I have one that assisted me in setting up power of attorney and things of that nature, but I didn't send anyone to check up on the living conditions at Pine Woods," Nick said. His words came out rapid fire and a new panic seized him.

Nick took up a light jog toward his mother's room, and it was the doctor who now lagged behind.

Nick entered the room and quickly eyed the two nurses that were alongside the bed where his mother lay. Her pearl-white hair was spread out gracefully across the pillow. The light that washed over her from above gave her a heavenly appearance. Her hands were folded across her stomach, and had the doctor not advised him otherwise, Nick would have assumed she was sleeping. *Peaceful.*

"Everybody get out now!" Nick said in a commanding yet controlled voice.

"Mr. Lawrence, what are you doing? You can't order them out. This is a treatment facility. There are tests to run and protocols to follow," Whitmore said, catching his breath as he spoke.

"Everything stops, and everybody needs to step out of this room," Nick reiterated.

Whitmore stood still, staring wide-eyed at Nick.

"We're going to be following my protocols now."

"Mr. Lawrence, I understand you're upset, but what are you talking about?" Whitmore asked exasperatedly.

"This room is now a crime scene."

Chapter 18

He heard a woman's voice speaking softly, but with an air of command in the hallway just outside the room. It sounded like Izzy. The thought was immediately dashed from his mind, knowing she would never again come through another door. In the threshold of the doorway stood his new partner.

Simmons approached, stopping a foot in front of Nick who was seated on a stool beside his mother.

"I'm so sorry Nick. How're you holding up?"

"As good as can be expected. Did you get hold of crime scene?" Nick asked.

"I called Cavanaugh and his team," Simmons said.

"I thought you guys didn't see eye to eye?"

"I don't see eye to eye with many people. And besides, Cavanaugh and Spangler have done the two most recent scenes. I'd rather keep some level of continuity in the processing," Simmons said.

"Makes sense," Nick said, staring at his lifeless mother.

He was devoid of emotion, an empty shell, running on autopilot.

His shoulders hunched at the massive weight that they carried, albeit an invisible one. Simmons placed her hand between Nick's shoulder blades. The sensation of her touch brought him into focus, and he turned his head up to look at her.

"It's not your fault," Simmons said softly.

The words stabbed at him with a ferocity more devastating than the knife he'd been impaled with months before. An intense tightness gripped his chest like an unseen trash compactor, squeezing his heart. Without thinking, and no words spoken, he slumped, crashing his head into Simmons's small waistline. Nick felt her arms shift to a loose, but welcome, embrace as his body shook uncontrollably. He resisted the emotional release and the discord conjured up an awkward whimper. The sound escaped his throat and its trumpeting brought him back from the abyss.

He sat upright and wiped his eyes, releasing her. Nick stood, creating more distance from Simmons.

"I'm sorry. I don't know what came over me."

"No need to apologize." Simmons eyed Nick as if evaluating him.

Nick nodded and rubbed his face, attempting to remove any trace of his collapse.

"I understand if this too much, too personal. And I won't judge you in any way if you want to come off the case."

"Are you kidding me?" Nick said with a steely look.

"I'm just saying that I would get it if you did. I took a leave of absence after the death of my parents. I had to hit the reset button. I almost didn't come back," Simmons said.

"Thanks, but no thanks," Nick said.

"All right. Just remember the offer stands."

"I appreciate it."

Nick broke eye contact with the green-eyed agent and cast his eyes downward, again taking in the sight of his mother's lifeless body. Seeing her in that bed and knowing that her last few days had been spent alone, without a visit from her only living son, sent a ripple of guilt that he knew would never leave. *I've failed you in life*, he thought, *but not in death.*

"Where'd they find it?" Simmons asked.

"In her hand. It fell to the floor when they checked for a pulse."

"Did they touch it?"

"Yes." Nick said.

"We'll still swab it for DNA and fume it for prints. Not that I have any expectation of finding anything but the nurses'."

"Have you ever before?" Nick asked without any trace of hopefulness.

"Not in twenty-nine bodies. So, I'm not holding my breath that your mother's coin will be the first."

Nick's eyes flashed with anger at the cavalier way Simmons referred to his mother, but it quickly subsided as he was aware of the hypersensitivity he was experiencing. She must've caught the look because she took a step back.

"I'm sorry. I didn't mean to dash any hopes," Simmons offered.

Nick sighed. "I'm just trying to wrap my head around this."

"That's why I offered to let you step away from the case. Get some perspective and come back at this thing fresh."

"That's not up for debate. I've got to see this thing through. Running away isn't an option," Nick said. He exhaled deep and long.

"Okay. I won't bring it up again."

"So, you're telling me that you've never got a hit on any of these coins? No leads?" Nick asked.

"Forensically, no. I've even tried to contact wholesalers and coin collectors but haven't generated any leads. Apparently, this coin, albeit old, is quite common. The tools used are also commonly bought. I guess if we found the Ferryman's tool we could positively identify it doing a comparative analysis of the striations, but that would be more for the case's prosecution than for locating our killer," Simmons said, rattling off the information.

"Okay."

Nick stared at the coin sealed in a small plastic ziplock bag resting on the nightstand.

"Why do you ask?" Simmons asked.

"I'm going to keep it," Nick said flatly.

"You're going to keep it? A piece of evidence?" Simmons asked.

"Like you said, it's not going to tell us anything we don't already know. So, I'm taking it." Nick said this with a finality and subtle firmness in his voice that did little to belie his conviction.

"Why?"

"As a reminder," Nick said.

Simmons did not answer verbally. She nodded, and her eyes cast him a solemn glance. Nick watched as she slid her delicate hand to her throat along the open collar of her cream-colored button-down shirt. Her finger tugged at the thin silver chain of a necklace draped around her neck. A pendant was exposed as she removed her hand, allowing Nick a clear view. The hobo nickel with an etched skull rested outside of her shirt between the slight rise of her breasts.

"My reminder," Simmons said.

"From your parents?"

"My father."

Nick reached over to the table without any further hesitation and picked up the bag containing his mother's death token. He opened the seal and his fingers dug out the coin. Nick slipped the silver coin into his pants pocket. He left his hand in his pocket and thumbed the raised features of the skull before letting it fall into the recesses of the pocket's cotton lining.

"I'm going to need you two to move unless you want to be in the shot," Spangler said, holding a large-lensed camera as he stood in the threshold of the door. The massive frame of Cavanaugh eclipsed the hallway's light as he stood behind, dwarfing the smaller crime scene tech.

"You guys are quick," Simmons said as she discretely tucked her pendant away.

"I figured we had to get over here before you agent types wrecked the scene," Spangler said.

Nick heard a hiss in Spangler's speech that he hadn't noticed before. It was more of whistle that followed certain syllables. Nick surmised that it probably was a byproduct of a deviated septum based on the crookedness of his bulbous nose. The effect gave his voice a lyrical lilt as he spoke.

Cavanaugh brushed past Spangler and approached Nick, clasping a large hand on his shoulder. "I'm sorry for your loss."

"Thanks."

"Anything you need on this, just ask," Cavanaugh said.

Nick nodded.

"We'll leave you kids to your work," Simmons said.

Nick saw Simmons bat her eyes at the large Homicide detective, taunting him slightly.

"I finished up the other scene from the dumpster. I emailed you the files including the photographs," Spangler said.

"Thanks Ed. I'll take a look when we get back to the office," Simmons said.

Nick squeezed his mother's hand one last time. The coldness of it seemed to linger fleetingly after he let go. Nick then turned to follow behind Simmons as she moved toward the white light of the hallway.

"There was a message," Spangler said.

Nick and Simmons both stopped, turning in unison to face him.

Simmons spoke first, "What message?"

"It was taped to his upper back. We didn't see it until we rolled him. It said, *Remember me? I am the soil that gave you root,*" Spangler said. "Creepy shit."

"Please tell me that it was a hand-written note," Simmons said wishfully.

"No luck. Letters cut from various publications. We're having it analyzed. Maybe we'll get lucky and the asshole forgot to glove up or glued down an eyelash."

"Let me know what you find," Simmons said over her shoulder, already moving in full stride again.

Nick paused for a fraction of a second. *Remember me?* He thought about the man in the alley. There was something familiar about him, but it was just out of his mental reach.

"Hey, did you ever get an identification on the guy?" Nick asked.

"Ran his prints. Chester Mullins," Cavanaugh answered.

"Shit," Nick said, and he took up a slight jog in the hallway, playing catchup with Simmons who was moving at a brisk pace toward the wing's exit.

Simmons turned as he approached.

"I think we've got our first break in the case," Nick said.

Simmons's eyes widened. "How so?"

"We need to get back to the office. If I'm right on this we may be able to predict the next victim," Nick said, barely able to contain his newfound enthusiasm.

His hand slid into his pocket and he rubbed the coin between his thumb and forefinger. A reminder of his failure. He wouldn't fail again.

Chapter 19

"It's late Nick. Let's hit the reset button and start again first thing tomorrow," Simmons said.

Nick looked at his watch. It was already past midnight. "I'm not much for sleep, and I don't think that's going to change tonight."

"I'm a bit of an insomniac too." Simmons gave him a gentle smile. Nick noticed she had a seductive quality when she softened her rigid exterior.

"Coffee?" Simmons asked.

"Might as well."

Nick stood up and stretched. His back cracked, and he exhaled with the release of its tension. He looked down on the conference table that was covered in a blanket of tattered manila case jackets.

"Somewhere in this mess is the answer. I know it," Nick said more to himself.

"I hope so," Simmons said striding out in the direction of the break room.

She returned a few minutes later with two porcelain mugs in hand. The steam rose, and Simmons placed a cup in front of Nick. World's Best Dad was stenciled on it. Somehow this mug had made its way into the community cabinet of shared items.

Simmons gave Nick a knowing smile. "Not yet, but soon."

Nick hooked his fingers in the handle and raised it to his lips, giving Simmons a half smile and wink acknowledging her comment.

"So let's walk this thing back and see if we can figure out his next move. Pentlow was part of your investigation. I get that piece. The Ferryman's way of reaching you. A loud statement to get your attention," Simmons said.

"Well he's got it. Undivided." Nick didn't look up from the open folder in front of him.

"Mullins. Well that is more concerning," Simmons said.

"I know. That case was six plus years ago. Actually, it was my first big one. I can't believe that I didn't recognize him in the alley."

"In your defense he looked like a wet bag of crap," Simmons said.

"True. Although, he didn't look much better six years ago."

"I guess life after Nick Lawrence hadn't been so good for Mr. Mullins," Simmons said.

"Good ol' Chester the Molester."

"Catching a child abduction conviction doesn't leave you with a lot of job opportunities on the outside. Especially when you're on the run," Simmons said.

"I still can't believe that he escaped from prison."

"Well, technically he wasn't at the prison when he absconded," Simmons added.

"True, but he was under watch at a counseling session."

"Where there's a will, there's a way," Simmons said.

"In my humble opinion, the world's a better place without him. To be honest if this asshole just stuck to killing pedophiles, then I don't think we'd be putting in this much effort," Nick said.

"That's the piece I don't get." Simmons ran both hands through her red hair and closed her eyes. "He's been near impossible to track. The homeless population is not too police-friendly and aren't likely to report anything. And most of them have been off the grid for some time with their legal names long since forgotten. People don't notice when they go missing. The Ferryman had always maintained a level of unpredictability in selecting his victims, and therefore he was like a ghost."

"And even more elusive if you add in the theory that he may be one of us?" Nick half asked, and half stated.

"He's got to be. He's able to avoid leaving any traceable evidentiary path. His pattern changes any time I've closed in on him. He also knew Pentlow's release date and was able to track down Mullins' whereabouts," Simmons said.

"I'm definitely starting to lean in that direction as well," Nick said.

The thought that his mother had just been killed was hard enough to swallow, but to think that it may have been done by someone in the law enforcement brotherhood sickened him. He clenched his fists and his body tensed, allowing himself to be momentarily lost in a self-absorbed rage.

"So, both Pentlow and Mullins had a proclivity for young children. Both were your cases, and both slipped through the cracks in the legal system," Simmons said.

"I'd say that summarizes it. Pentlow hadn't technically slipped through the cracks. His case was pending trial. He was able to bond out, which did surprise me because of how high the judge had set it. I personally didn't think he'd ever see the light of day."

"You didn't know?"

"Know what?" Nick asked.

"That he turned State's witness on a murder case."

"What do you mean? What murder?"

"His cellmate happened to make a jailhouse confession giving Pentlow intimate details on a cold case homicide of a prominent business man's daughter. He was going to walk on the rape case. Maybe not scot-free, but he'd be looking at a reduced sentence or time served with lifetime on the sex offender registry. That's what I'd call slipping through a pretty big crack in the justice system," Simmons said.

"I didn't know. Shit. That asshole had an eleven-year-old girl tied to a bed. And they were going to release him back into the wild?" Nick asked rhetorically.

"It's bullshit all right. Enough to make somebody take the law into their own hands."

Nick stopped sifting through the files. Simmons's comment derailed his train of thought. He felt her eyes burning a hole in him. Nick knew that there was no way that she knew about his vigilante spree against Simon Montrose, the ring leader of a sex ring. But he felt like she knew, and therefore he'd fallen victim to the subconscious reaction referred to as the spotlight effect by interrogators. His cheeks flushed, and he refused to make eye contact for fear that she'd see right into the darkest depths of his soul.

"Nick?" Simmons asked.

"Sorry. I was just thinking—about my mom," Nick said, hating himself for covering his emotional tracks with his mother's death.

"I know what you're going through. Trust me," Simmons said.

Nick looked up. People always say *I know what you're going through*, but in this particular case Simmons had survived a similar tragedy, and he knew that she meant it.

"Thanks," he muttered softly.

"Mullins, too, wasn't going to be spending the next twenty years in prison. He escaped during an off-site psych session. Now he's dead," Simmons said.

"That other part of his note about being the soil. It makes sense now."

"How do you mean?" Simmons asked.

"I agree that this Ferryman is law enforcement, because he knew that Mullins was my first case. My career and reputation grew from that investigation," Nick said.

"Well folks, we have a believer," Simmons said, raising her hands as if she were testifying at Evangelical revival.

Nick smiled and returned to his solemn stoicism.

"And now my mom," Nick said softly.

"Yes, she's outside the pattern. We know he wanted to get your attention. And now we know that he wants to hurt you," Simmons said, pausing to take a sip of her coffee. "What we don't know is why."

"Okay. Outside of my mother's death, the Ferryman seems interested in killing off any of my former arrestees."

"Correction. Only ones that have beaten the system. Beaten your case," Simmons said.

"Well, if you're right, then that will help narrow things down a bit," Nick said, suddenly focused, rifling through the stack.

"How so?" Simmons asked.

Nick was silent as he focused his undivided attention on the pile before him. He stopped when he found what he was looking for. He pulled a thick folder and slammed it atop all the others. "Here's the next victim."

"What do you mean? How would you know that?" Simmons asked with a furrowed brow.

"You said that he's targeting cases where the suspects have managed to beat my case?"

"That's the pattern I'm seeing," Simmons said.

"Well, here it is," Nick said with an air of confidence.

"Here what is?" Simmons asked.

"The only other case that I know of where the bad guy didn't get the maximum sentence."

"So, you're telling me that in your years in sex crimes you've only had three cases fail?" Simmons asked, cocking her head to the side in feigned disbelief.

"I'm good at what I do," Nick said confidently and without a trace of cockiness. It was plainly a statement of fact.

"That's impressive. Only three?" Simmons asked again.

"There was a fourth. A human trafficking ring run by a guy named Montrose. He had good lawyers and lots of money. He paid off some lower level guys in his organization to take the fall. It worked. He walked away free and clear."

"So, there were four?" Simmons asked.

"*Were* being the operative word. Montrose is dead. He was killed in some gangland-style shootout at his home. As I recall, it was deemed to be an organized hit," Nick said, ensuring that his words did not betray his secret to the profiler standing before him.

"Organized hit?" Simmons asked.

"They said it was done with military precision. Montrose and four members of his crew were taken out without a single report of shots fired. A rather difficult task to accomplish since his house was located in a rather exclusive neighborhood. I guess someone higher up in the food chain didn't like the possible fallout of his potential risk of testifying. Or maybe it was some turf war. Either way it remained unsolved," Nick said.

"I guess that closes that door and leaves us with who?" Simmons said.

"Antonio Scalise," Nick said, sliding the folder across to Simmons.

Simmons took up the chair nearest to Nick. Her knees rubbed lightly against his as she leaned in to peruse the documents. He caught a whiff of lavender.

"What's his story?" Simmons asked.

"Child pornography."

"What happened to the case?"

"It was pretty tight, but there was a screwup at the evidentiary level. The hard drives seized from his home went missing from evidence during the initial phase of the trial. Prosecution backed down even though we had digital copies of the data retrieved. They wanted the originals. Scalise's attorney won the suppression hearing, and without our files, the case was lost at trial," Nick said.

"Evidence went missing? That's not something that happens too often."

"They investigated it and found that Scalise had a distant cousin in the bureau. Long story short, the cousin is currently doing time, but the drives were never recovered," Nick said.

"Did Scalise miraculously die by a random drive-by or act of God?" Simmons jested.

"Not that I know of."

"Well then, it sounds like we'd better get our asses over to talk with this creep," Simmons said.

"It's almost one o'clock in the morning," Nick said.

"I don't think he'll mind the visit once we tell him why we're there."

Nick then remembered that he hadn't called Anaya back after leaving the hospital earlier. Looking at the time, he deemed it far too late to call now. He would wait until morning. The thought of her being far away from Austin gave him some comfort.

Chapter 20

It was quiet except for the crunch of their footsteps as they approached the double-wide trailer that was home to child porn connoisseur, Antonio Scalise. Simmons banged loudly on the door with a total disregard for the time of night. The sound resonated in the stillness. Nick cringed at the sound's dissonance to the quiet of the impoverished housing area. A neighboring home's light kicked on and a silhouette peered out through the blinds.

A white flickering light emanated from within Scalise's trailer. A television was the only provider of discernable light and could be seen through the loosely hung torn screen of a filthy window. Simmons banged again, this time with more force than before. The sound carried and a dog barked in the distance.

"Whoever the hell is banging on my door in the middle of the night better have damned good reason!" a thick voice yelled from within.

They waited. Neither agent spoke. Nick heard the creak of a chair and the distinctive sound of a recliner's foot rest being slammed into place. Footsteps banged the unstable movement of the man's gait. One foot louder than the other, but each one struck the flooring with enough force that shockwaves reverberated along the thin off-yellow vinyl siding of the trailer's walls.

The door swung wide. Antonio Scalise stood staring at the two agents through the dirt-covered screen of his closed storm door. His large frame and massive gut occupied the poorly lit threshold. His greasy black hair was matted down and looked as though he hadn't showered in days. And by the rank odor trickling out its assault on their sense of smell, Nick guessed it may have been more like a week.

Scalise squinted hard, ping ponging his eyes back and forth between the agents. His gaze held a fraction of a second longer on Simmons and with each pass his glance focused more on what lay beneath her neckline. Scalise pushed the thick-lensed glasses higher up the wide expanse of his nose and into place. Nick observed as the amplified eyes of Scalise widened at the sudden recognition of the man who'd arrested him several years ago.

"You son of a bitch! You come to my house in the middle of the goddamned night! I better see some kind of warrant! Harassment! I'll sue you blind! When I'm done with—I'll have both your badges—," Scalise bellowed. His rapid fire verbal onslaught took a physical toll and his ruddy cheeks flushed with blotches of red.

"We're here to protect you. So, lower your voice and let us in," Nick said.

"You're not coming in my house! That's the last thing you'll ever do. You can tell me whatever it is you've gots ta say from where you're at st stan-d-d-d-d-in," Scalise ranted, spitting the words.

Nick had forgotten Antonio's little quirk. He suddenly remembered Scalise had a stutter. An impediment worsened at moments of intense anger or frustration. Nick had exploited the weakness numerous times during his four plus hours of interrogation with the corpulent pervert.

"I don't like seeing you again either, but we have reason to believe that someone is coming for you. You're not safe," Nick said.

"You're going to p-p-pr-pro-t-tect me? You're the asshole that t-t-tr-tried t-t-to ruin my life!"

"Not much to ruin, you fat sack of crap! You don't want our help? Fine. Good luck with what little time you have left on this earth," Simmons interjected.

Nick turned, smiling broadly at the fiery redhead. He was awestruck at her tenacity and wit, saying the words he'd wanted to say but didn't.

He whispered, "You've got a hell of a bedside manner. Thankfully we're on the same team."

Simmons smiled at the backhanded compliment but never broke eye contact with the flustered obese man.

"Wait. I don't understand. Who's out to get me? I didn't do nuthin' to nobody," Scalise said.

"I'd beg to differ, but we're not her to talk about your past inclinations," Nick said.

Nick noticed that Scalise seemed to reset after the admonishment by Simmons. The blotchiness of his meaty jowls faded back to the unhealthy glow of a man not accustomed to sunlight. He was impressed at her ability to redirect and had the suspicion she'd used this tactic in the past with equal success.

"We'd be happy to explain," Simmons said.

Antonio Scalise stared blankly.

"It'd probably be a better idea to have this conversation inside and out of the earshot of your nosy neighbors," Nick added.

"I guess that makes sense. But don't be snoopin' around my damn place!" Scalise snarled.

Nick smiled, "Don't worry Antonio; we've got much bigger fish to catch right now."

Scalise looked back into his trailer and hesitated only for a second before shoving hard against the handle to the storm door. The door latch clanged and the hinges grinded a resistant screech. The door looked as though it were going to separate from the frame as it swung wide, and the unhinged pneumatic door closer failed to stop the momentum. The door banged loudly against the outside of the mobile home.

Scalise muttered something about meaning to fix his door as he retreated into the trailer, allowing the agents to enter his cluttered abode. The three now stood in what could only be described as the living room. A strong aroma hung in the air. A pungent combination of cat piss and cigarettes attacked Nick's nostrils. He took shallow breaths to negate the sour ingestion of tainted oxygen, but to no avail.

"Tell me what's going on and be quick about it," Scalise said.

"Trust me, we don't want to be taking up any more of your precious time than needed," Simmons said sarcastically.

"We're tracking a killer and the long and short of it is we believe he's targeted you," Nick said.

"Me? Why?" Scalise asked, scratching flakes of dandruff out of his scalp.

"This killer has taken an interest in Agent Lawrence."

"Good." Scalise spat the words as he eyed him intensely.

"No. Not good. Because the killer isn't going after Agent Lawrence directly. He seems to be going after people involved in Agent Lawrence's cases. In particular, people that he's arrested who beat the system. You fit a short list of people that meet that criteria, Mr. Scalise," Simmons said.

"You bastard! First you destroy my life and then you b-b-b-br-bring this d-d-down on me?"

"We're not going down that road again, Mr. Scalise," Simmons said firmly.

Scalise huffed and began teetering back and forth as if suddenly unbalanced. To Nick the overweight pedophile looked like a weeble-wobble punching bag of his childhood. Nick felt a sudden desire to punch the wide face of the man in front of him. He refrained from indulging and let the rage subside as he watched several trickles of sweat race down the man's forehead. It was cold in the trailer but apparently not to the four-hundred-pound man.

"So, what are you going to do about it? Do you have a plan to catch this asshole?" Scalise asked.

"Watch and wait," Simmons said.

"Watch? And what? Wait for him to kill me?"

"Watch you. Watch your house. And yes, wait," Nick said.

"That's it? A killer's out there somewhere and you're just going to sit around on your asses and wait? My tax dollars hard at work," Scalise said, unnerved.

Simmons made a show of surveying the home. "I don't think your tax dollars are doing much for our salaries."

"Screw you lady!" Scalise fired back.

"As to sitting around waiting. Well, that's the thing. We don't know who this killer is. So, we really have no choice," Simmons said.

"Jesus," Scalise said through labored breaths.

"How many doors?" Simmons asked.

"Huh?" Scalise asked, lost in thought.

"How many doors does this place have?"

"Oh. Um… two."

Scalise wiped the moisture from his brow and transferred it to his stained gray sweatpants, adding to the collection of other stains. "Only one locks. The front."

"So, the back door doesn't lock?" Nick asked.

"I haven't gotten around to fixin' it yet. It's on my list of things to do."

"Been busy cleaning?" Simmons said sarcastically, surveying the filth.

"Screw off!" Scalise said weakly.

"Just lock the door after we leave. We're going to be close by keeping watch," Nick said.

"Don't change up your routine. We don't want to tip our hand. Not sure we'll get another opportunity like this." Simmons turned to leave.

"So that's that? I don't get a gun or something?" Scalise asked, mashing his wet palms together nervously.

"No Antonio, you do not get a gun. But don't worry, we've got that covered," Simmons answered.

Nick said nothing, eyeing the fat man intently and recalling the depravity of his unpunished crimes. He turned and followed behind Simmons.

"P-p-pl-please keep me safe," Scalise called out softly as the door closed.

Nick let the heat from the Jetta's vents warm them as it idled. He'd positioned the compact car kitty-corner across from the dilapidated home of Antonio Scalise. The Jetta's black exterior gave them an additional layer of concealment coupled with its stealthy position between an overfilled dumpster and broken-down tow truck. The location gave him a three-point visual of Scalise's double-wide to include both the front and back doors. The poorly maintained, dirt covered road leading into the trailer park would serve as an early warning if anybody approached in a vehicle.

"Rock, paper, scissors to see who gets the first watch?" Simmons said.

"No need to bother. I've got it," Nick replied.

"You really don't sleep much?"

"Nope. Not since Afghanistan."

Simmons nodded, but remained silent. Nick appreciated the quiet acceptance and respected her for not pressing him further on his statement.

"The Ferryman always makes his move at night?" Nick asked.

"Every case so far. With the exceptions for the outliers like your mother," Simmons said.

Nick's lips pursed, sealing in the pain of his mother's death. He closed his eyes and tried to clear the thought from his mind. He felt Simmons fingers trace over his right hand that rested on the balled plastic of the car's stick shift. She gave him a quick squeeze, gentle but firm enough to convey its meaning. A gesture of solidarity between the two who, until recently, had not shared so much in common. Nick opened his eyes and gave his new partner an appreciative smile. Simmons retracted her hand and reclined in the passenger seat, preparing to settle in for a long night.

Nick stared at Scalise's pitiful residence. He watched as the flicker of light from his living room television danced out into the dark night. The low rumble of the engine in idle mixed with the heavy breathing of the woman next to him, an indication that sleep had taken her.

Chapter 21

The morning light forced its way through the windshield of the black Jetta, immediately elevating the temperature of the compact car's interior compartment. Being awake when night gave way to day never came naturally. The transition was not subtle, and it caused his stomach to churn. The noise of it amplified by the quiet caused Simmons to stir. She rolled her body toward his and the movement exposed the subtle cleavage peeking out of her loosely buttoned shirt. The necklace she wore was exposed, and the dead eyes of the Ferryman's token stared emptily back at him.

"Jesus, how long were you going to let me sleep?" Simmons yawned, looking at the digital display on the dashboard.

Nick shrugged. "Looked like you needed it more than me."

"What's that supposed to mean?" Simmons wiped the sleep from her eyes and squinted as she turned to face him.

"Nothing. It's just that you passed out pretty fast and slept hard. I figured your batteries needed recharging."

Nick stepped out of the car. The ground had a light coating of frost, painting the brown dirt of the road in patches of white that looked like mold on stale bread. The ice crunched as it was compacted under his weight. Nick stretched, arcing his torso while reaching skyward with his arms. He inhaled deeply, allowing the cold air to revitalize him. A couple vigorous twists of his body relieved the tension in his back and neck, signified by the audible popping sounds. Satisfied that he was fully adapted to morning's call, Nick reentered the vehicle.

Simmons was sitting up and smiling at him.

"What's so funny?" Nick asked.

"It's just crazy to me that a big guy like you picked this little car."

"It came my way after a joint case with the DEA. A drug seizure vehicle. I figured it's a little less conspicuous than a Crown Vic or Impala." Nick patted the top of the dashboard like he was praising a dog. "She's been good to me so far. Although not the most spacious accommodation for long nights of surveillance," Nick said.

"Well, I think it's safe to say that Fat Tony will be around to walk the earth for at least one more day," Simmons said.

"Fat Tony? Geesh, for a behaviorist you really don't mince words."

"Life's too short for political correctness. Plus, I've got a reputation to live up to. I don't want to lose my hard-earned nickname."

"Nickname?" Nick asked turning to face her. "Oh, I've gotta hear this!"

Simmons chuckled. "Cherry bomb."

Nick laughed out loud. "Cherry bomb?"

Simmons shrugged sheepishly. "That's what they affectionately call me. Cherry bomb."

"Who's *they*?" Nick asked.

"Pretty much anyone who's ever worked with me. I'm actually surprised it didn't follow me here to Austin. Hell, in the Dallas area even the local cops use it."

"I'd be lying if I said it didn't fit," Nick said, still smiling broadly.

"You haven't seen anything yet," Simmons said with a coy smile that teetered on the brink of being flirtatious.

Nick maintained his smile for only a moment longer before returning to his typical stoicism.

"I did a lot of thinking last night trying to piece this thing together," Nick said.

"And what'd you come up with?"

"Zilch. Nada. I can't think of one person I know in our profession that'd be capable of doing what this asshole's done."

"I know. That's probably the biggest stretch for me too," Simmons said as she fiddled with her pendent briefly before returning it to the recesses of her shirt. She buttoned her blouse, sealing away the necklace while simultaneously masking her gentle curves.

Nick averted his eyes but caught a knowing glance from Simmons.

"Drop me at the office. I'm fresh faced and bushy tailed. You, on the other hand, are not. I want you to take a few hours to decompress and sleep."

"But—," Nick started.

"But nothing. No more arguing. I need you to be at your best so that we can get some fresh perspective on this. Don't worry, you're not going to miss anything crucial. I'm just going to be doing a little administrative housekeeping.

I've got to pop over and meet up with Spangler to pick up the files on Mullins and your mother."

Nick's head spun at the mention of his mother. Dizzied by the thought, he realized Simmons was right. There was no way he'd be effective later if he didn't take some time and shut down for a bit.

"All right. You win," Nick conceded.

Nick eased the Jetta forward from its hiding place, making his way around the dumpster and onto the dirt roadway of the dead-end street that was home to Antonio Scalise. The crunch and pop of the wheels' rotation along the unpaved surface sang out the end of their first night's surveillance.

Nick plodded his way up the wooden steps of his front porch. The cold air nipped at his exposed skin and he gripped the wooden railing for balance. He entered his quaint, yet adequate, home and was greeted by the contrasting warmth. The thermostat read 72, but this temperature had little to do with the setting and more to do with the natural warmth provided by the Texas sun. The living room was brightly lit by the tendrils of sunlight penetrating through the horizontal slits of the cherrywood blinds.

He felt the exhaustion of the last two days take hold and his body went slack. Nick thoughtlessly tossed his jacket onto the back of a chair, foregoing the hook that was only an arm's reach away, and collapsed face first into the couch's expanse. His motor functions, operating on delay, did not seem to respond to his mental commands as he fumbled with great effort to retrieve the phone from his pocket. He wanted to call Anaya and check in.

After much more effort than should've been required, Nick successfully yanked the phone free. The coin, the Ferryman's gift, slipped out and rolled across the marbled white tile, spiraling until it came to a stop, landing faceup. Nick stared as the orbital cavities of the etched skull stared blankly back at him. The weight of this silent staring contest bore down on him heavily. His eyelids fluttered in futile resistance and then succumbed. The phone fell from his hand, the call never placed, as he slipped into a deep sleep with the hope of awaking from this nightmare.

Chapter 22

Nick shot up, slamming the ridge of his foot against the oak leg of the coffee table. A line of drool snapped its connection from the left side of his face to the indented floral-design couch pillow. He vigorously rubbed his head, disoriented to his surroundings. It was dark. The small hand on the wall clock was on the five and the seconds ticked by noisily in the stillness. Nick had no idea if it was morning or night. He illuminated the backlight function on his G-shock watch. The numbers glowed their green response, 17:03.

He rubbed his foot, taking away the sting of his clumsy awakening. Nick retrieved the phone from its resting place on the floor and the coin that lay next to it. He depressed the button on the side of the black Samsung. Nothing. It was dead. He discontentedly rose from the couch and staggered to the kitchen. He plugged in the phone, started recharging the dead battery, and clicked the power button on the Keurig located nearby on the counter. With the whir of the heating coils beginning their task, Nick shuffled off toward the bathroom, disrobing as he strode.

The steam from the shower's warm water cleared his fog. Refreshed, he stepped from the bathroom into the dark bedroom. It took a moment for his eyes to adjust but he caught something move by the bed. Nick dove toward the dresser where he had placed his duty weapon.

A flash filled the room as the lights came on, the contrasting brightness blinded him.

"Nick?"

Nick was caught off guard by the sound of Anaya's voice, and he lost his footing and stumbled, tripping clumsily over the end of the bed. He popped up like he'd landed on a springboard. The towel he'd wrapped around his waist came undone during his acrobatic dance across the bedroom. He stood facing Anaya in nothing but his birthday suit.

"I missed you too, babe, but maybe we could say hello first before jumping into the sack," Anaya said playfully.

Nick hunched over, bending slightly at the waist and placed his hands on his knees while he allowed a moment for the adrenaline dump to dissipate.

"Holy shit! What—I... why?" Nick babbled.

"I never heard back from you last night after you told me about your mom. I panicked and rebooked my flight for this morning," Anaya said.

"Why didn't you call me?" Nick said, but realized as soon the question left his mouth that he knew the answer.

"I did! I called you this morning. Multiple times. It went straight to voicemail. What was I supposed to think!" Anaya paused, but Nick could tell she wasn't done and didn't want to interrupt. "I was worried sick. I thought the absolute worst. I mean—your brother..."

"I'm so sorry. I—just... it's been an insane couple of days," Nick stammered.

Nick saw Anaya's face soften.

"How'd you get home from the airport?"

"I grabbed an Uber."

He picked up the damp towel from the floor and secured it once again, pulling it taut around his waist. Nick swiftly crossed the distance between them in a few long strides and took Anaya in his arms. The water rolled from his shoulders onto her coat that was still carrying a hint of coldness from the outside air.

Nick said nothing as he pressed his face deep into the soft brown skin of Anaya's neck. He held tight and never wanted to let go, like clutching on to a lifeboat in a sea of sharks.

"I love you Nicholas Lawrence," Anaya whispered in his ear.

The words slipped in past his rugged exterior and tore at the darkness. He melted into her embrace allowing her to heal him. Even though Nick towered over her in size, he suddenly felt small in her arms. He liked the power she had over him.

"Never do that to me again!" Anaya whispered with a deep-rooted intensity, making it seem more like a yell.

"Never do what?" Nick asked.

"Never disappear on me."

"Okay. I'm sorry," Nick said.

"Not good enough. Promise me!" Anaya pleaded.

Nick pulled back and looked into the dark eyes of the woman he loved. "I promise."

Looking at her, he allowed his shock to subside. A new thought caused his eyes to widen. His mind focused as panic filled him.

"You shouldn't have come back! You should've stayed with Mouse in Michigan!"

"I couldn't. Not with you here all alone. Not after your mother—"

"It's not safe! I'm not sure I can protect you," Nick said. His voice quivered. He placed the palm of his hand on her stomach. "Protect both of you."

"What do you mean protect us?" Anaya asked.

"I didn't tell you when I called. It wasn't the right time and I didn't want you to worry more than I already knew you would."

"What are you talking about Nick?"

"My mother's death wasn't a heart attack. She didn't die of natural causes," Nick said emphatically.

Anaya's eyes widened. "What?"

"I told you there was a real threat to me...to us, and to any member of my family. You were safe in Michigan. You were away from this lunatic. I had this under control or I was at least working toward that end! Now, with you here, I'm at a tactical disadvantage."

Anaya didn't speak. She pulled away from Nick and dropped her head, breaking eye contact with him. He felt the air cool on his wet skin, replacing the warmth provided by her body. She gingerly took a seat on the edge of the bed and slowly began taking a long, deep breath.

"Are you okay?" Nick asked.

Anaya didn't answer but instead held up her right hand with her index finger extended, indicating she needed a minute. He'd never seen her react this way. Nick knew Anaya to be as tough as they came. She'd endured more than most could fathom, and he'd spent countless hours listening intently to her stories of her traumatic childhood ravaged by the world of human trafficking. Seeing her reaction to their current situation worried him greatly.

"Breathe. Nice and slow. Try to keep your head up and focus on a specific point in front of you. Inhale through your nose and exhale slowly through your mouth. This will help control your breathing and keep you calm," Nick said evenly.

Anaya nodded, but didn't look up. Her breaths came in rapid succession, each one more shallow than the previous.

"I'm going to get you something to drink. And a damp rag," Nick said, a trace of panic slipping into his inflection.

"Nick," Anaya said, muffled by her ragged breathing. "Something's not right."

Nick dashed to the kitchen, his bare fleet slapping the tile floor, as he nimbly navigated the narrow hallway. He swiped his cellphone off the counter, ripping it free from the charger. Running back toward the bedroom, he depressed the power button, bringing the device to life. The phone's cacophony of vibrations shook in his hand, alerting him to the barrage of missed calls and text messages.

His heart skipped a beat when he entered the bedroom to see Anaya curled in the fetal position on the floor. Her arms were wrapped tightly around her knees and her body trembled uncontrollably. She looked at him with eyes wide in terror as sweat moistened her brow. In the infinitesimal amount of time he'd taken to retrieve the phone, Anaya had gone through a complete metamorphosis into a huddled mess.

"Jesus!" Nick gasped, falling to the floor and cradling her head against his bare thigh.

"The baby." Her voice labored to project the words. Her breath followed in quick shallow bursts.

Nick placed her head back down on the plush throw rug jutting out from under the bed. He jumped up and threw on a pair of pants and t-shirt. Forgoing all else, he scooped up Anaya into his arms. Although Anaya was petite, the strain of her dead weight caused Nick's muscles to ripple with exertion. He cradled her as gently as he could. Her neck flopped loosely and her eyelids flickered rapidly as her eyes rolled into the back of her head. Nick shuffled to the door with as much speed as he could generate, snagging the keys to the Jetta before pushing out into the gloom of November's early dusk.

The dashed dividing lines of the highway blurred into one continuous white trail as Nick blazed forward, pushing the capabilities of the Volkswagen's economical five-cylinder motor. He'd called ahead to the hospital to alert them of his impending arrival and given them a description of Anaya's current condition. The nurse he'd spoken to was calm, and tried, without success, to reassure Nick. She advised they'd be standing by.

Nick smacked the curbing as he entered into the lane denoted for Ambulance only. Anaya groaned softly in the back seat at the jostling torque of the car. Nick's bare foot stomped hard on the brake and the small four-door slid to a stop directly in front of the Emergency Room entrance.

As promised by the person he'd spoken to on the phone, several medical personnel were clustered inside the threshold of the sliding doors and poured out toward the car once it came to a complete stop. A team of people in colorful scrubs hustled over and began speaking to each other. The words held no meaning to him and were barely audible above the beating of his heart. Two large men in turquoise scrubs hoisted Anaya gently onto the gurney. Anaya remained curled in the same position she'd been in on the floor of their home. In a blur of movement, she was swept away by a rainbow of chaos.

A nurse approached holding a clipboard pressed tight against her chest. She was heavyset with blue eyes. There was tranquility in her eyes that naturally induced a sense of calm. "Park your car over there. It's supposed to be for doctors but nobody checks," she said, pointing to a row in the parking lot. "I'll be inside when you're ready. I'll get you over to the waiting area."

Nick froze at hearing the words *waiting area*. Just three days ago it was Izzy and now here he was again, this time with Anaya.

"Are you okay?" the nurse said, eyeing him with concern.

Nick looked down at his bare feet and realized he must look like a lunatic. "Yeah. Sorry. I just—um… I'll be right back. Thanks."

Nick jumped in the car and parked in a spot marked ER Doctors Only. He jogged back to the entrance and entered the warmth of the lobby.

The blue-eyed nurse stood by a large leafy plant and smiled lightly. She held up a pair of light brown hospital socks. "These'll be better than nothing."

Nick quickly slipped them on, hopping on one foot for balance.

"Much appreciated," Nick said gratefully.

The rubber ridges on the bottom of the socks gave Nick some much needed traction as he followed the nurse along the recently buffed floor. She was his Sherpa, guiding him along the uncharted territory of the hospital's webbed corridors. She brought him into a room with a physical layout much like the one he'd waited in with Declan and Val. Unlike that room, it was crowded and loud. Even amidst the noise and commotion of the other visitors, Nick felt isolated. And for the first time in a very long time, he felt something, an almost foreign sensation. Fear. Palpable, and wholly undeniable.

Chapter 23

"I don't know. Still waiting," Nick said into his phone as he paced around the room.

"That's the worst part. Anticipation takes its invisible toll. How are you holding up?" Simmons said.

Her voice echoed and Nick noticed a slight delay.

"Do you have me on speaker phone?"

"No. Why?" Simmons asked.

"My end's got a little echo."

"I'm in a stairwell. Give me a second, I'm just leaving Spangler's office," Simmons said.

"Anything?"

"Yes, but I think it can wait."

"Bullshit! All I've been doing for the last hour is waiting. Give me something to occupy my mind. Something to distract me," Nick pleaded.

"There was a letter left back at Pine Woods."

"Letter? What letter?" Nick asked.

A fleeting thought graced his mind that his mother had written him something in one of her more lucid states. Words that would give closure to a soured end. He knew it was wishful at best and discarded the idea before it took root.

"The *lawyer* left it with the receptionist on his way out. She'd been off shift when things broke bad. She had put it aside and notified us when she came back to work today. I called earlier, but your phone was off. Figured it could wait."

"What did it say?" Nick asked.

Nick heard a rustle of paper and a pause as Simmons cleared her throat.

"Not sure this is the right time, Nick."

"Not sure there's such a thing," he mumbled. "Just read it."

"All right. Same format as the one found on Mullins. Cut paper lettering and the like." Simmons cleared her throat again. "*I ended your beginning. Soon you will know mine.*"

Nick was silent.

"Nick?"

"Yeah?" Nick was despondent.

"Let's get this son of a bitch," Simmons said.

"I'm all in."

"I never had any doubts," Simmons said.

"What's the next step?" Nick asked.

"Well, I'm planning on heading back to Fatty McGee's humble abode in a little bit," Simmons said.

Her blow at Scalise's expense tripped up his train of thought, allowing him to release the tension strangling him. Nick snorted a laugh.

"There's no way I can leave Anaya tonight. I've got to be here for her."

"I get it, and please trust me when I say I totally understand. I can go it alone tonight. I've got my big girl pants on," Simmons said.

"I don't like it."

"What's not to like? If the Ferryman shows up, I can throw a little reunion party for him. I've got a shiny pair of bracelets I'd like to give him," Simmons jested.

"Take another person with you tonight. I insist," Nick said.

"I didn't know you cared," Simmons gushed mockingly.

"Seriously, take someone from the office."

"Who? You want me to grab Salazar? A new kid like that would be more likely to shoot me than the bad guy."

"Let me think for a minute," Nick said dismissively.

"Anyone you trust enough if something breaks bad?" Simmons asked.

Nick immediately thought of Declan but knew that was out of the question. His next thought was of Izzy and it saddened him profoundly.

"Nick? You still with me?" Simmons asked.

Nick snapped out of his spotty funk. "Yeah, sorry. Kemper Jones. He's with APD. Solid as they come."

"The name's familiar," Simmons said.

Nick said. "I think you met him on Pentlow's scene."

"He's the one that tipped you off to me? The little birdie that whispered in your ear?"

Nick didn't answer. *Damn she was quick.* Cheryl Simmons missed very little.

"I'll take that as a yes," Simmons said.

"I trust him. And that's something I don't say about many people in this world."

"You're an interesting guy, Nick Lawrence."

"How so?"

"An office full of agents, and when asked who you trust, you name a local," Simmons said.

"You're not the only one that has a hard time finding a partner," Nick replied.

Simmons laughed into the phone.

"I'll send you his number, so you can make arrangements with him. Give me a couple minutes so I can get him up to speed," Nick requested.

"What you really meant to say is you need a couple minutes, so you can warn him about the crazy redheaded bitch he's about to spend eight hours with?"

"He's already afraid of you." Nick chuckled. "I just need to let him know he's about to spend the night in a car with you."

"Sounds more like you're setting me up on a blind date."

"If you're interested, the way to his heart is through a prime cut of smoked brisket," Nick said.

"I'll keep that in mind."

"Do me favor and don't go getting yourself killed."

"I'll do my best. And don't you go worrying over little ol' me. You've got more than enough on your plate right now. I'll keep you posted if anything breaks," Simmons said.

"Watch your six," Nick said earnestly.

"Will do. I hope everything turns out okay for your girlfriend and the baby," Simmons said softly.

"Thanks. Me too," Nick said, ending the call.

The commotion inside the waiting room died down as people departed. There were noisy utterances of their dashed hopes or joyful elations as news of their loved one's prognoses were delivered. Nick tried to temper his disdain as he waited for an answer. Time sluggishly passed, minutes felt like hours.

A clean-cut man with hair the color of brushed steel entered from a secure door marked Medical Personnel Only. He wore a pearl white lab overcoat over teal scrubs and walked directly toward Nick, bypassing all remaining guests in the waiting room. The man's eyes, intensely focused, locked on Nick's. The doctor's wrinkles etched into the olive skin of his face marked his life's experiences, equal parts pleasure and pain. Nick held on to the hope that the news soon to be delivered would not fall into the latter category.

"Mr. Lawrence?"

"Yes," Nick said. He tried to sound confident, but what little reserve he had left in his emotional tank had drained and the effort came out flat.

"Anaya's going to be all right," the doctor said.

"What about the baby?" Nick asked, steadying himself for the blow.

"Absolutely fine."

"Fine? Did you say fine?" Nick asked.

He'd heard the words, but his mind had already prepared for the worst and therefore didn't comprehend them. Nick staggered and caught himself by grabbing at the nearby lip of the window sill, almost knocking over a potted plant.

"She had a panic attack, but that was it. She and the baby are all right."

"What about the stomach pain?" Nick asked, still processing the information.

"Apparently she hadn't eaten since yesterday. There was some intense cramping caused by some gastrointestinal distress. We put her on an electrolyte drip that will help give a quick boost. Food is already on the way up from the cafeteria."

"I just thought she—the baby..." Nick trailed off without finishing the words.

"I'm sorry that we kept you waiting as long as we did. We had to run a battery of tests to ensure that everything was all right with both mom and child."

"Run all the tests you need to. I'm just glad they're going to be all right," Nick said, righting himself, his panic quelled.

"It must have been terribly frightening for you. Anaya tells us that this is your first child?" the doctor said, giving him a warm smile.

Nick watched as the creases around the doctor's eyes became more pronounced.

"Yes, it is. In a week of worsts, this brought me to full blown panic mode," Nick said.

"Well, let's not keep you two—correction, you *three* apart any longer. I'll take you to her now," the doctor said.

"Thank you. For everything."

Nick stayed in stride with the doctor as they moved down the hallway. Nick's rubber-bottomed socks gave a slight squeak as he kept pace with each step. The silver-haired doctor stopped outside of room 131, the door already open. The doctor stepped aside, tipped his head in a slight bow, and opened his arm as if he were Vanna White revealing the final letter. "I'll leave you two alone."

Nick gave the doctor a hearty handshake conveying his appreciation, before turning his attention to his supine Anaya. He crossed the room to her bed in three elongated steps. His large frame cast a long shadow over her petite outline in the bleach-white cotton sheets as he leaned over to place a kiss on her forehead.

"Sorry," Anaya whispered.

"Baby, you had me so worried," Nick said through his pressed lips. "Please never do that to me again. I don't know what I'd do without you."

"I was a mess after hearing about your mom. When you didn't call I freaked out. And then the morning came. I thought of your brother. I don't know what came over me. I…" Anaya rambled. The monitor adjacent to her bed beeped the slight elevation in her heart rate.

"No. It wasn't your fault. This one's all on me. I should've called. I should've been better about keeping you in the loop. I got focused and lost sight of what's really important."

"I know how you get on a case. I should've let you be and trusted that you'd handle it."

"I guess my past track record with you might cause you some concern," Nick said, tapping the scar on his hip.

"You do have a tendency to get the worst of things." The yellow specks in Anaya's dark eyes twinkled as she smiled up at him. "I mean, I don't know too many people who have survived getting shot, blown up, and stabbed."

"Maybe people should learn their lesson and realize that it's a lot harder than it looks to kill me and just give up trying," Nick said, laughing at his own joke.

As soon as he'd said the words his mind returned to his current predicament. Nick knew the Ferryman would never give up, but took solace in the knowledge that neither would he. Nick took additional comfort in Simmons's tenacity.

A clang of a cart striking the door frame interrupted their quiet interlude, and the thin black orderly pushing it announced, "Chow time!"

Nick slid the roll-away dinner table over Anaya's midsection and then adjusted the bed setting, bringing her from a supine position into an upright, seated one. The man slid the tray containing a covered dish and plastic-wrapped utensils. "Bon appetite!" he said before retreating out of the room and down the hallway to his next delivery.

Anaya lifted the blue plastic cover allowing for the trapped steam to escape as beads of condensation trickled out. "Yummy," she said sarcastically.

"Eat your mystery meat and lima beans so I can get you out of this place," Nick said playfully, but with an underlying truthfulness.

"Okay." Anaya gave him an exaggerated pouty smile.

"I'm going to step into the hallway and make a couple calls," Nick said.

"You're leaving me?" Anaya asked nervously.

"Not tonight," Nick said moving for the door. "Not ever."

Nick saw Anaya giving him a quick once-over, pausing at his shoeless feet and the hospital-issued fashionable footwear. "Nice outfit," she joked.

Nick laughed, giving a quick strut and turn. His best attempt at a runway model turn was met by the lovely smile of Anaya, the soon-to-be mother of his child. For an infinitesimal amount of time he'd forgotten the dire circumstances they faced and allowed the darkness to be replaced by something else... happiness.

"How's it going?" Nick asked.

"Good as gold, my friend," Kemper Jones said. His voice was garbled.

"Are you eating?"

"Of course. It's a damn stakeout." Jones paused, swallowing the bite of blackened meat imprisoned in his mouth. "Long nights of sitting by a dumpster in a nasty trailer park go perfectly with a plate of burnt ends."

Nick heard the detective laying on his thickest West Texas accent for added effect. He knew that is was done for show and probably more so to grind the nerves of Simmons, sitting next to him. "Don't eat too much. I can't have you falling asleep out there."

"Don't worry about me. This is fuel for my investigative gas tank. You just take care of

Anaya and let us handle the grunt work," Jones said.

"Seriously Kemper, I owe you one," Nick said.

"For you, anything," Jones replied.

"Hey, keep me posted if something breaks. I'll have my phone on me."

The second call was one he'd been meaning to make since leaving Connecticut but hadn't had the time or the mental reserve to handle. It only rang once before the other end picked up.

"Hey bro. I've been waiting to hear from you," Declan said.

"I know. Things got crazy out here, and fast."

"You okay?"

"Have arrangements been made yet?" Nick asked, trying his best to avoid the disastrous combination of the words Izzy and funeral in his dialect.

"Saturday."

"Shit! That's less than two days. No way I'm going to be able to make it back," Nick said, running his free hand through his hair.

"That makes two of us. I'm not going to be able to make it either," Declan said.

"What? Why?"

"I'm actually heading to Ohio as we speak," Declan said.

"What's in Ohio?"

"Some Arian Brotherhood compound in the woods. ATF has got their panties in a bunch about it. They've worked up a massive OP plan and HRT is on point. Hopefully, it won't end up being another Branch Davidian scenario," Declan said cavalierly. His telling was delivered in the same matter-of-fact manner of somebody talking about picking up eggs at the grocery store.

"That sucks."

"Won't be so bad. I heard Ohio is beautiful this time of year."

"Not that. Izzy. She'll be alone when they put her in the ground," Nick said.

"There'll be family there."

"But not us."

"I've missed more funerals than I've attended in my life and buried more friends than I'd ever care to count. Guys like us say goodbye in a different way," Declan said.

Nick sighed, relinquishing the guilt. "Agreed. When the dust settles in our lives we'll have our own vigil to send her off properly."

"Damned straight! I'll bring the whiskey." Declan cleared his throat. "Be safe, brother."

"You too. I'll see ya when I see ya," Nick said.

He ended the call. The wall outside Anaya's room had a slight give to it as he leaned the full weight of his body against it. With Izzy gone forever and Declan unavailable, Nick felt isolated and alone in a battle against an enemy without a face. He was stepping forward into uncharted territory.

Anaya lay peacefully against the raised bed's mattress, staring contentedly at her empty plate as he reentered the room. The combination of intravenous drip and hospital food reinvigorated her, changing her complexion from the murky paleness of earlier and returning it to her natural muted light brown. Nick looked at her and saw his future. He wouldn't let anything harm her or their baby.

Chapter 24

"You have one hell of a surveillance routine," Simmons said.

The container precariously balanced on Jones's protruding gut as the Austin detective drove his sauce-covered fingers into the pile of meat.

"You sure you don't want some? You're really missing out," Jones said, holding the charred triangular tip of beef in her direction.

"I'll pass," Simmons said, giving a leery eye as Jones methodically licked the sauce from each finger. "You look like a walking crime scene."

She watched Kemper stop his cat-like cleaning routine to evaluate the variety of red stains decorating his button-down.

"Maybe white isn't your color," Simmons jested.

Both laughed, and then Jones returned to finish off his cleanup. A storm door clamored and one of Scalise's neighbors stepped into the light of their porch. The embers of a cigarette splashed orange across the woman's face. She looked around, wearily scanning the surrounding pitch black of the night.

"I'll take first watch. You can sleep off your dinner," Simmons said.

"Sounds good to me." Jones took a long pull from his Styrofoam cup. A loud slurp followed by a squeak emanated from the cup as Jones swiveled the orange plastic straw in a final attempt gather up any remnants of the Dr. Pepper hiding among the melting ice cubes. A final gulp trumpeted the end of his feast.

"If I start to snore just hit me. It's what my ex used to do."

"If you snore, I'm going to put you in that dumpster." Simmons thumbed in the direction of the large brown metallic bin shadowing their gray Taurus.

Jones gave a hearty chuckle. "Good luck lifting me," he said, patting his ample gut.

Simmons smiled. "I'm stronger than I look."

"Well, I'm heavier than I look."

"Get some rest big fella," Simmons said, winking.

"Ya know? Ya ain't so bad," Jones said, adding his colorful West Texas charm. He gave a tip of his invisible Stetson before reclining the seat and closing his eyes.

Simmons redirected her focus back to the double-wide that was home to Antonio Scalise. The female smoker had disappeared into her trailer, and once again the only contrast to the dark was provided by the flicker of the heavyset pervert's television. She stared into the abyss of the surrounding night while the labored breathing of her rotund companion served as this evening's background music.

The longer you stand still the more invisible you become. Darkness always helps, but movement is the quickest way of exposure. The car had been idling by the dumpster for a while. The rise from the engine's exhaust was a telling sign of its location, but in the cold it would be too much to go without the heater. Weakness provides advantage. Edging forward inch by silent inch, the Ferryman had moved to the rear door of Scalise's deplorable home. No reaction in the unmarked fed car.

Tonight's mission would need to be quick. No time for games with the house under surveillance. But rules were rules and a message needed to be sent. The puzzle was almost assembled. Soon they would understand.

The rust on the hinge of the exterior storm door was visible in the low light conditions, indicating the years of neglect. A delicate hand and slow pull negated the noise. A sharp wind cut through the park rattling lose shutters and clotheslines. The clatter created an additional mask to the entrance. The loose knob of the interior door turned easily and with a firm push the door opened. The house was under surveillance, but this slob hadn't managed to lock his door. It's like Scalise had invited death to come.

The interior was peppered by a landmine of clutter. Each step contained the pitfalls created by the morbidly obese Scalise, who obviously did very little in the way of cleaning. Navigating without making a sound through the dark kitchen was more difficult than expected. The volume of the television blaring from the other room helped blanket the crunch of stale cereal that couldn't be avoided. Light danced out of the living room and assisted the

Ferryman in maneuvering around the dining table, teetering with magazines and ashtrays. The unbalanced pile was a madman's version of Jenga.

No time for games. *All work and no play,* he pouted.

The Ferryman silently slipped behind the unaware fat man who was bobbing his head in a fitful battle with sleep. The rolls of fat on his neck jiggled with each recoiled nod of his head.

The knife was already balanced in the Ferryman's hand as a quick assessment was made for the angle of trajectory for the first and hopefully only strike. The decision made, the blade raised with the thumb bracing the end of the handle.

Just as the strike was about to be delivered, the television show cut to commercial and in the split second of screen darkness during the transition, the image of the Ferryman and the glimmer of the knife in hand was reflected back at the unprepared Antonio Scalise.

"What the—" Scalise started to say.

His incredible weight precluded his ability to react from the chair, which was molded tightly to his massive body. The knife struck downward into the right side of the man's neck between two protruding rolls fat, adding resistance to the weapon's bloody withdrawal.

No other words were uttered. The only sound competing with the incoherent banter on the television was that of the gurgling of Scalise. Agonal gasps seeped out his final plea.

Back to the door from where the Ferryman had just moments ago entered, a quick pause on the crooked stoop of the rear entrance. The Ferryman's eyes adjusted to the dark and peered hard in the direction of the dumpster across the dirt-covered street. No movement from the Taurus. Satisfied, the Ferryman stepped slowly down the two steps and disappeared, becoming part of the night.

Chapter 25

"Wake up!" Simmons yelled, shoving Jones.

The slumped mass of the detective snorted and then muttered something inaudible. She shook him again, this time more violently. A loud nose erupted that sounded like a combination of both a snore and a choke. He lurched upright, eyes wide with his head on a swivel.

"What the hell is goin' on?" Jones blurted.

"Movement. Back door," Simmons said, pulling her gun free.

"I don't see it. Where?"

"I swear I just saw something!" Simmons said.

She was already moving from the car and into the cold. The butt of her pistol hugged tightly to her sternum as the muzzle pressed ahead, seeking its target. Simmons hunched over, lowering her profile as she moved quickly toward Scalise's dwelling.

"Shit!" Jones blurted.

Kemper Jones fumbled to open the door, stepping on his empty container of barbeque as he tumbled out the side door of the Taurus. Somehow the Styrofoam container latched on to his left foot, and Jones shook it as he jogged to keep up with Simmons, who was already on the move ahead of him.

The two moved quickly in the direction of the back door. Simmons hopped up the two rotten wood steps to the landing with the nimble grace of a Romanian gymnast, pausing at the threshold of the door. She looked back at Jones who nodded. Understanding the non-verbal signal, Simmons jerked open the storm door and pushed the interior door hard with her foot. She shoved her small frame into the tight space. She wedged her right foot against the door, preventing it from bouncing back on them. Jones noisily clamored up the steps and followed behind her.

They quickly visually cleared the kitchen area and moved fast toward the living room. They heard a strange sound. A hiss and gurgle, comparable to the sound of a clogged drain fighting against the introduction of water.

Simmons entered the living room and was able to visually clear the small space, the visual assessment made easier by the cast of the television's light. With no threat located, she holstered and approached the dying Scalise. Terror was carved into those beady eyes.

"Get a towel! A rag! Something!" Simmons yelled over her shoulder to Jones.

Jones threw a grease-covered dishrag he'd found under a pile of magazines. Simmons caught it in the air. She pressed hard at the wound. The towel did little to stop the flow and was saturated within seconds. Simmons hands were wet. Scalise squirmed as if trying to look past Simmons toward the kitchen area where Jones was standing. And then, an instant later, he stopped moving altogether. His dead eyes looked up at her as if making some final unsaid petition.

Simmons stepped back, looking for somewhere to wipe the dead man's blood from her hands. She looked down at her clothes and realized that was a moot point. In her hasty attempt to clot the flow emptying from the gravely wounded man, she'd managed to cover much of herself in Scalise's arterial spray.

Jones was speaking, but she comprehended none of it.

Her temporary auditory exclusion dissipated as she distanced herself from the dead man, and she heard Jones say, "I called it in."

"Damn it!" Simmons yelled. She lurched toward the front door, ripping it open.

She bolted onto the front stoop and withdrew her gun again, frantically scanning the darkness. Nothing moved and the only sound she heard over the wind was Scalise's television.

She held the position for a moment longer, but knew in her heart that the Ferryman had eluded capture once again. The only chance they had to bait him just finished bleeding out on a worn-out La-Z-Boy recliner.

Chapter 26

The rhythmic drumming sound grew louder, ripping him from sleep and rattling his brain like a jackhammer. His right eye opened quicker than his left in the discord between synaptic command and neuromuscular response. The green glow of the numbers slowly came into focus. 2:03 a.m. The drumming sound started again. His cellphone shook on the mahogany end table, the same end table that had once been his parent's prior to the sale of their family home. The caller was unrelenting, and the phone alerted receipt of the incoming call, spinning slightly under the power of its vibration.

Nick grabbed the phone midvibration and swiped madly at the green icon, seeking refuge from its annoying interruption to his hard-fought sleep.

"Nick, you awake?" Simmons asked eagerly.

"I am now. What's up?" Nick asked, sitting up and placing his feet on the throw rug at the base of the bed.

His toes curled, gripping the fluffy vines of fabric as he looked back at Anaya. She was sound asleep, undisturbed by the sound of his voice and commotion of his movements.

"It's Scalise. He's dead," Simmons said.

"Dead? What? You guys were there. Are you and Jones all right?" Nick asked desperately. Terrified that his mind was incapable of handling the news of another loss in his life.

"We're fine. A little shook up is all. I'll fill you in when you get here. Meet us at his trailer park," Simmons said.

Nick hesitated for a brief second as he watched the gentle rise and fall of the sheets that lay over his beloved Anaya. At the hospital he'd made a promise that he wouldn't leave her tonight. The confliction between his duty to her and his obligatory compulsion for justice gnawed at him.

"Okay," Nick said hesitantly.

"You sound a bit unsure. Everything good on your end?" Simmons asked.

"Yeah. She's all right. So is the baby. We got back home around midnight. She's sleeping now," Nick whispered.

"Good to hear. So, you're on the way? Right?" Simmons asked again.

"I'm up and moving. See you in a few." Nick said this cradling the phone between his shoulder and ear as he quietly pulled open a dresser drawer. He grabbed an armful of clothes and stepped out into the quiet of the living room to dress, removing any chance that his bumbling would wake Anaya. Nick jammed a piece of gum in his mouth to remove the sour taste of sleep. The mint flavoring made the night's air feel colder as he stepped out from his house and away from Anaya, leaving his promise broken. The note he'd left by her nightstand, containing the words, *Sorry, I had to step out for a minute. I'll be right back,* did little to lighten his guilt.

Nick arrived on the scene, driving down the unpaved dirt road he'd been on the previous night. The trailer park looked nothing like it did before. Large flood lights were now posted on two opposite corners of the double-wide mobile home belonging to Scalise.

Nick slithered through the crowd of neighbors gathered at the edges of the bright yellow tape, taking stock of their attire. Most, if not all, were wearing jackets over some variety of sleepwear, indicating their affiliation to the neighborhood. It was unlikely the killer would go through so much trouble to blend in. None of Nick's internal sensors tripped any potential alerts to a threat among this group.

People craned hard in a frantic attempt to catch a glimpse of what caused the horrific end to their neighbor, searching for an answer to the swarm of police that had taken over the small patch of land belonging to the now-dead Antonio Scalise.

Kemper Jones stood in a dark corner outside of the cone cast by large mobile floodlights. He teetered at the edge of the crime scene tape, but on an area far away from the onlookers. His face was illuminated by a soft warm glow with each pull of a cigarette. Nick observed the rate at which his friend was puffing away. The rapid-fire piston of his arm as he devoured the cigarette did little to alleviate his anxiety.

"Those things will kill ya," Nick teased as he approached.

"Gotta die of something. Lot better way to go than some. And definitely better than the way he went," Jones said, gesturing in the direction of the trailer's back door.

"You okay?"

"Yeah. Not my first dead body," Jones said between puffs.

"Not what I asked," Nick asserted.

"I know. And yes, I'm good to go. Just pissed at myself for falling asleep," Jones said.

"That's how these operations work. Taking turns on the watch. One person sleeps while the other keeps eyes on," Nick said.

"I know but maybe we would've been quicker to react. Four eyes are better than two."

Nick nodded and looked around, "Where's Simmons?"

"Inside talking to Cavanaugh," Jones said, taking another long pull before flicking the glowing butt out into the darkness. "She's fearless. I like her."

"I know. Me too. She'd have to be, after everything that's happened to her," Nick said.

"What do you mean?"

"This asshole killed both her parents a few years back. Tried to finish her off too."

"Jesus, I didn't know," Jones said.

"Neither did I. Not sure it's something she likes to talk much about. I can't really blame her."

Nick ascended the two rickety steps leading to the back door. The creak of the metal storm door announced his arrival.

"Look who decided to join the party," Simmons said, smirking at Nick.

"Better late than never," Nick said.

"Interior photos are done," said a tall bald man wearing the distinctive blue of an APD crime scene windbreaker.

Nick didn't recognize the tech.

"Thanks. Get the exterior and photograph the crowd too. Maybe this sicko came back to watch the show," Cavanaugh said. His voice boomed loudly, intensified by the confines of the small space.

"Where's Spangler?" Nick asked.

"Couldn't get hold of him," Cavanaugh said.

"That's not like him. Doesn't he live for this shit?" Nick said. "I don't think I can recall a recent scene that I've been on without him."

Cavanaugh chuckled. "Maybe he finally got himself a life."

Nick laughed. The large Homicide detective stepped out the front door making enough room for Nick to navigate around the kitchen table. Scalise's body was contorted, sprawled between the recliner and the floor, as if he had turned awkwardly to greet Nick. The faded light blue of the living room carpet was now stained dark with blood. His dead eyes stared up at Nick.

"Please tell me you got a glimpse of him," Nick pleaded to Simmons.

"I wish. I didn't even know that it was him. I saw something by the back door. No details. I couldn't even tell if it was a person. I just saw a different shade of darkness, like a shadow moving inside of a shadow."

"Damn it!" Nick hissed.

"Maybe if this fat slob had ever changed a light bulb in his godforsaken life that back-porch motion light would have caught him," Simmons said, frustration seeping out.

Nick realized Simmons was holding a plastic bag, containing a white piece of paper.

"Is that what I think it is?" Nick asked optimistically.

"Yup," Simmons said.

"And?"

"*You look but do not see. Now there's just you and me.*" Simmons recited the words with poetic intonation.

"He's taunting us," Nick said, grinding his teeth.

"No more cases to tie us to the pattern. No more bait. We've got nothing." Simmons balled her fist. "We're now back to square one and no closer than we were a few days ago."

"Not so sure about that," Nick said.

"How so?" Simmons asked.

"We've still got me."

"You?"

"He's got to come for me sooner or later. We just have to get a leg up on this bastard," Nick said.

"Well that's failed us so far," Simmons said dejectedly.

"We're definitely missing something. Not sure what, but there is a link to all of those cases. All of those dead men. I know it's there. We just have to find it."

"Are you heading back to the office?" Simmons asked.

"Yes. I'm going to look over everything again. Put some fresh eyes on this thing," Nick said.

"Okay. I'll meet you there in a bit. I've got to get cleaned up," Simmons said.

For the first time since he'd entered the residence, Nick took notice of the woman standing before him. There weren't many areas on the clothing clinging to her small frame not covered in Scalise's blood. The sanguine darkness of the dried fluid stood in disparity to the brightness of her hair.

Chapter 27

Nick sat alone in the conference room. The only injection of noise since he'd arrived had been made by him and his love affair with the Keurig machine in the break room. Since then, the only sound had been the flipping of voluminous paperwork as he ravaged the files, convinced the answer was buried within.

He'd removed everything from the stretched oval of the conference table except for four case files: Montrose, Pentlow, Mullins, and Scalise. He scoured the write-ups and looked at every supplemental report searching for a name. Someone who was at each of those scenes. Someone who knew the system. A cop.

Nothing clicked. There were officers, investigators, and agents tied to one or two of the case investigations, but none that he saw were linked to all four. Nick gave a disgruntled grumble, rubbing his head vigorously in the hopes of stimulating his thought process.

He then spread out photos from each of the scenes. Hopeful the answer was there. The atrocities of these savage men and the brutality of their sickness captured on film. Nick compared the crime scene photos taken at the time of each man's arrest and grouped them with the photos from each man's death, minus Scalise's scene which was still being processed.

He stared at the evidence sticker affixed to the bottom right of each photograph denoting the tech who took it.

Nick's eyes widened, and he jumped up from his seat, knocking over his chair. His eyes danced from case file to case file, picture to picture. There, neatly written at the bottom of each photo, was the same name: Ed Spangler.

Nick looked up at the dry erase board set along the back wall of the room. Notes had been tossed up over the last several days. Simmons's profile annotated in red marker. Male. Short: 5'03-5'05". Age 30-50. Cop?

Cop?

Ed Spangler was all those things except a cop. He was a tech, but he had been there all along in the backdrop. Every scene. Every photo.

In haste Nick fumbled with his phone almost dropping it. He banged his fingers on the screen calling Simmons. It rang five times before going to voicemail.

Nick left a frantic message, "Hey it's me. I figured it out! I know who it is—the Ferryman. Spangler—it's freakin' Ed Spangler. Call me as soon as you get this!"

It was unlike Simmons not to answer but Nick assumed that she was either in the shower or had fallen asleep after washing off Scalise's caked bloodstains. He looked at the time. It was already 6:00 a.m. He realized that Anaya might be awake soon, and he didn't want her to find him not home. There was still time to make it right or at least give her the illusion he'd kept his promise. The last thing he needed right now was for her to have another panic attack. Nick dashed out of the conference room leaving the disarray of files as a testament to his mind's unique system of reasoning.

Traffic was light leaving the city and Nick arrived home well under his normal commute time. He quietly slipped the key into the lock, turning it cautiously. He entered, hoping that Anaya was still resting. He didn't want to wake her if she was. Nick stood unmoving after closing the door, listening intently to the silence.

Satisfied he'd returned home before Anaya had awakened to his absence, Nick crept to the back room of their small ranch styled home and into the bedroom. Dawn's light had delivered its pale welcome, making it easy to see into the room. The bed spread was turned down and an indentation was left where Anaya had slept, her slender form pressed into the old, non-resilient mattress. There was no sound. No shower running. No lights on. A nothingness that stirred a panic so deep that Nick momentarily froze.

Nick called out to her, "Anaya?" Soft at first and then booming louder, "Anaya?!"

He willed himself to move and ran from room to room hysterically searching for Anaya. She was gone. He'd failed her. Failed to protect her. Failed to keep his promise.

Nick raced to the door and out into the brisk air. He descended the stairwell in a mighty leap. He turned the ignition to his Jetta and then stopped before pulling out from his parking space. He had no idea where she was. He had no idea where he was going. His phone vibrated. A lifeline thrown at this most despairing of moments.

"He's got her!" Nick gasped into the phone. His voice cracked, revealing his lack of control and desperation.

"Slow down. Who's got who?" Simmons asked.

"Ferryman. He's got Anaya!"

"What? I don't understand."

"Did you get my message about Spangler?" Nick asked frantically.

"No. I just saw that I missed your call. I passed out after my shower," Simmons said.

"It's Spangler. The Ferryman is Spangler!" Nick yelled.

"Ed Spangler, the crime scene tech?"

"Every scene. He was at every one of my scenes. He's been there the whole time. In the background, but always there nonetheless." Nick tried to control his breathing and reset his calm. Without it he'd be useless.

"I'll call you back in a minute," Simmons said.

The call ended, and Nick sat. The heat from the vent began to fight back against the cold, and the fog from his panting dissipated, no longer visible.

His phone alerted to Simmons's incoming call, and he answered before the first ring ended.

"I've got a ping going on Spangler's phone. It hasn't moved in a few hours. I'm going to send you the address," Simmons said.

"I'll meet you there. Call it in. Send everybody!" Nick said.

"Already did. I told the locals to stage if they arrive before us. I'm moving now. I just hope we're not too—" Simmons said.

Nick ended the call not wanting to hear the end to of that sentence. The phone buzzed its receipt of the address Simmons had forwarded. He forwarded it to Jones and then dialed his number.

A thick groggy voice answered in deep drawl. "Hey, I was just about to give you a call. I did some digging and—"

"He's got Anaya! Meet me at the address I sent you!" Nick said into the phone, hanging up without waiting for a response.

He punched it into the map function on his phone and gunned the car in the direction of Spangler's last known location. The navigation map gave a twenty-three-minute arrival time. He planned to cut that time in half, revving the engine as he accelerated west out of Georgetown.

Chapter 28

Nick's Jetta hugged the turn as he rounded his way into the posh Cedar Park neighborhood. The ornate exteriors of towering houses merged into a blur as he doubled the posted speed limit of the quaint suburb. A fleeting sense of déjà vu gripped him as he slammed to a stop behind Simmons's idling Taurus. A long, crushed-stone driveway led up a gentle rise to the impressive house. Standing there looking up, he recognized he'd seen this house before. He'd not only seen it but been inside it on two uniquely separate occasions. This would be the third and, hopefully, final visit.

Nick withdrew his Glock and exited the car. Simmons, as if on cue, exited hers. The two met in the middle with guns pressed down at the low ready.

"Where's the cavalry?" Nick asked. "I figured they would've been here by now."

"Not sure. I called it in. They should be here any minute," Simmons said, looking back and forth between Nick and the white-bricked exterior of the house.

"We don't have a minute!" Nick said through gritted teeth.

"My thoughts exactly. Let's put an end to this once and for all!" Simmons said, looking down at her duty weapon.

"This asshole is never going to see the inside of a courtroom," Nick hissed. His eyes gauged the reaction of his new partner.

"Agreed," Simmons said, reciprocating his anger.

They made a low-profile approach in tandem, shuffling quickly along the grass in an effort to minimize the sound of their footsteps. The light glared off the glass of the windows, masking any visual of the expansive home's interior.

"I know this house," Nick whispered as they moved.

"What do you mean?" Simmons asked quietly.

"Simon Montrose, the sex trafficker. It's his house. Same house I arrested him in and the same one he was killed in," Nick said.

"Why here?" Simmons asked.

"Not sure, but whatever the reason it's definitely not by coincidence. Nothing has been thus far," Nick said ominously.

Simmons nodded and the two continued pressing forward.

Stacked against the white brick of a gabled arched doorway, Nick pressed the latch. The door was unlocked. Nick looked back into the intense green eyes of Cheryl Simmons.

"I'm following your lead," Simmons whispered. "You move and I'll be right on your ass."

Nick pressed his thumb down on the ornate doorknob, a bronze lion's head with the tongue for a latch. The tension of the dark wood door released as the weather seal was breached, making a miniscule suction sound. Nick put his palm on the center of the hand-carved stained marble oak of the door and pressed firmly. The door swung wide. The cloud cover kept the sky a washed gray, but the home's numerous windows allowed for what little light there was to fill the vastness, bouncing off the reflective marble flooring.

The point of no return reached. No hesitation in the fatal funnel. The two agents made a smooth entry into the foyer. Simmons keeping her word, drafting off his hip as she snaked to the right, opposite Nick. Both took up points of aim, visually clearing as much of the main room as possible without any unnecessary progression forward. They stopped and listened.

There was nothing to indicate anybody else was inside. Then a scream. Nick immediately recognized the echo of Anaya's voice as it bounced off the high walls that extended up to the vaulted ceiling. The reverberation of the sound disoriented the pinpoint of its origin. Another voice, less clear, and more mechanical cut through the ensuing silence following Anaya's desperate plea. The deep rhythmic pulse of the Ferryman's unfeeling voice inflamed Nick's rage.

Nick looked at Simmons and she nudged her chin in the direction of an open spiral staircase that led to the second floor.

Without a word Nick moved up the winding steps, taking them two at a time. He ascended with reckless abandon. His elbows tucked against his ribs, and his gun slightly cantered in the center of his chest enabled him to maintain a tight but stable shooting platform, even at his enraged pace.

Nick crested the landing as Anaya released another bloodcurdling scream. The sound exploded in Nick's ears, causing him to stumble awkwardly as if it had physically impacted him. Simmons stepped up, grabbed his shoulder and righted his leaned position.

The direction of the sound was more clearly identifiable in the closed space of the second-floor hallway.

The only unnatural light seeped from underneath a paneled wood door located at the end of the hallway.

Anaya's words stole the air from Nick's lungs. "Please don't! I'm pregnant! My baby! No!"

A robotic voice muttered a response, unclear above the whimpers and screams of his cherished Anaya. Then a loud crack like that of a bullwhip cut the words short. Nick ran toward the door, disregarding any attempt to tactically mask his approach. The screams beaconed him, propelling him forward at an inhuman pace.

Nick didn't break stride hitting the door with his left shoulder at full speed, his mass multiplied by his speed. The force had a devastating effect on the decorative interior door, splintering the frame. The door flung wide, scraping the floor as one of the upper hinges snapped.

Unable to control his momentum, Nick tumbled onto the hard tile, smacking his head.

A dizzying pain shot across his forehead temporarily blinding him. Nick shook off the discomfort as glittering stars fluttered across his vision. Nick spun on his back, scanning for Spangler.

His eyes were still watering from the impact when he saw Anaya in a chair in the center of the sparsely decorated room. Her head slumped forward and her body limp. Nick fought the urge to vomit. Standing beside her was a short figure in a black hooded sweatshirt. A dark mask covered his face and the outline of his eyes was barely visible through the red tint of his wire-rimmed glasses. In his right hand was a short whip. His left held tightly onto Anaya's chair back.

A loud groan roared from the masked man. Nick pivoted, still on his back, and took aim between his knees at the dark figure.

Two loud bangs rang out from his right as Nick watched, connecting the pieces of the adrenaline-filled millisecond. His mind put the moment into a slow-motion replay and he watched as the second shell casing pitched free, tumbling away from Simmons's weapon as the payload was delivered to the intended target.

Nick followed the path of her aim and saw that the masked figure was slumped forward, kneeling awkwardly next to Anaya. His hand still gripping firmly the back of the chair.

Anaya sat unmoving and silent.

Nick exhaled deeply, suddenly aware he'd been holding his breath. He gasped as he scampered across the floor on his hands and knees. Her body was tied firmly to the chair, totally immobilizing her. Only her head was unrestrained and flopped indiscriminately as Nick ran his hands over her body, searching both visually and tactilely to assess the damage. He totally disregarded the man slumped to his left. Nick's only care in the world was that of his love, Anaya Patel.

He pressed his index and middle fingers hard into the side of Anaya's neck waiting for desperately for an answer. The faint bump of her heartbeat gave Nick the strength to quell some of the dread and allowed the bile in his throat to recede.

Nick then turned his attention to the hooded man slumped next to him. His eyes observed the black zip tie securing the man's gloved hand to the back of Anaya's chair. Nick tried to understand the significance of it but was totally baffled.

The two holes in the center of the sweatshirt left little question, but Nick pulled the mask down to check vitals. The glasses fell to the ground revealing the dead eyes of Ed Spangler. His mouth was covered in the same silver duct tape as Anaya's.

Nick's mind reeled at the strangeness of this visual inconsistency. He spun to relay this strange turn of events to Simmons and instead found himself facing the squared barrel of a department-issued Glock 22.

Chapter 29

"You?" Nick questioned, as his rage exploded.

He sprawled backward from Simmons's muzzle, climbing on the body of the crumpled crime scene tech.

"Sometimes the things we do have repercussions, Nick. Sometimes you cross paths with someone who bites back," Simmons said.

"I have no idea what the hell you're talking about!"

Nick glanced at his gun. It was on the floor a few feet away on the opposite side of Anaya's chair, where he'd put it when checking her pulse.

"Not a chance you get to it before I put a round in your head. But if you think you're quick enough, then by all means, please go ahead and try," Simmons said curtly.

He put the thought out his head for the time being. He was left with little option but to stall.

"Why? I'm not seeing any of this. Cheryl, I—what did *I* ever do to you?" Nick asked.

"You took my last bit of humanity," Simmons said.

"You're not making any sense! I've never met you. Not until this week. What the hell are you talking about?" Nick asked, fearing that Simmons was in some type of psychotic break and worried that if he pushed too hard too fast she would snap.

"I've always had a taste for it. As long as I can remember," Simmons said.

"Taste for what?"

"Death."

Simmons looked at the whip in Spangler's hand. Nick followed her gaze and realized that it wasn't a whip but was in fact a willow branch, barbed with nubs from where the leaves had been stripped off.

"Daddy tried to help. He tried to make me better. Beat it out of me. With a branch much like that one there," Simmons said.

Nick noted that Simmons spoke with a reverence for either her dad or the whip, or both. Regardless, it was creepy and left him uneasy.

Nick said nothing. He listened trying to find an angle.

"It didn't take. Daddy died, and then there was nobody left to help me with my problem," Simmons said with a strange curl of her lip.

"I thought—you said—your parents were killed a few years ago," Nick stopped himself realizing nothing she'd told him before was true.

"Nope. Never knew mom. She abandoned me early on. Dad stuck around. He was good to me. Even the beatings were done out of love."

"So, you killed him?" Nick asked, buying time.

"Not me. He was killed by a local homeless man when I was thirteen. Same year I got put into foster care. Same year I got pregnant." Simmons paused as if giving way to deep thought. "A lot of firsts for me that year."

"Jesus. How the hell did you ever pass the psych?" Nick asked.

"I'm really good at reading people. Even better at manipulating them." Simmons smiled and her eyes gave a glimmer of crazy. "You know that saying takes one to know one?"

Nick nodded.

"How do you think I got handpicked for the Behavioral Analysis Unit? I can track 'em because I am one."

"Shit." Nick muttered.

"Poor little Nick. So lost. So hurt."

"I still don't understand what any of this has to do with me," Nick said.

"You will. I'll make sure of that. Otherwise, all of this would've been for naught."

The tape covering Anaya's mouth pulsed, and a murmur slipped through her tightly sealed lips. Her head began to sway, indicating her distressed return to consciousness. Nick saw the flutter of her long eyelashes.

"Perfect timing!" Simmons exclaimed. "Your sweet little Anaya will get to hear about the real Nick Lawrence. The Nick that I'm all too familiar with."

"She knows everything about me. So swing away," Nick said. His eyes flashed with anger.

"Not everything. No, not everything. But she will!"

Nick was silent.

"Do you think she'll still love you when this is over?" Simmons asked sarcastically.

Nick ignored the question and scooted closer to Anaya, and in doing so, closer to his gun.

"Move again without my permission and I'll shoot her," Simmons said matter-of-factly.

Nick stopped, settling in to his new position a few inches closer but still too far to give any potential advantage. He stared intently at Simmons, evaluating the woman he'd gotten so close to over the past few days. Seeing her now, the red of her hair framing her face and giving her a wildness that only fueled the fire of his boiling rage.

"I know that look. I know it all too well. You want to kill me?" Simmons chided.

"More than you'll ever know," Nick retorted.

Simmons chuckled. "I doubt that. I know a thing or two about wanting to kill a person."

"I get it now. You're a sick person. But what I don't get is what this has to do with me?"

"Simon," Simmons said.

"Montrose?"

Simmons's head nodded up and down, moving slowly for added effect. Didn't you find it the least bit strange that his house is where this little journey ended?" Simmons asked, never taking the gun off him.

"I did. And I still do."

Anaya stirred again. This time her head lifted. Tears rolled down the soft curved line of her cheek as she surveyed the room. She eyed him warily, the terror percolating just beneath the surface. Nick received her silent plea for help.

"Good to have you back with us," Simmons said mockingly.

Nick admired the fight in Anaya's moist eyes as they narrowed in defiance of the armed woman standing above them.

"You may be turning that mean old gaze on your boyfriend in a minute when I let you in on his little secret and tell you what he's been up to."

Nick shrugged and shook his head, fending off the implication.

"I hope that baby of yours is still okay," Simmons said, smiling down at Anaya's stomach.

"What did you do?" Nick seethed.

"There it is. That's what I want. Do you feel that? That deep anger surging at the mention of your defenseless unborn child?" Simmons hissed.

Nick said nothing. His breathing accelerated, and he could feel the tingle of adrenaline prickle along his skin.

"I can see it in your eyes. You are beginning to understand my pain."

His ears thumped with the beat of his heart, nearly drowning out her words.

"A child's death carries a never-ending flow of pain. You gave me that gift and I've given a lot of thought on how best to repay your generosity," Simmons said, contemptuously.

Nick's brow furrowed in thorough confusion at the madness.

"I carried Simon Montrose in my womb for nine months. Nine months!" Simmons boomed through clenched teeth.

"Oh shit," Nick said.

"Oh shit is right. Starting to make sense to you now isn't it, Nick?"

Anaya's head swiveled back and forth between the two, her brow knotted in confusion.

"Of course, I didn't get to name him. The State took care of that for me. And, like me, he was born a product of the broken social service system. Even though he moved through the pipeline into a closed adoption, I managed to track him down. Like any loving mother, I kept an eye on him." Simmons said with a contented smile. "I watched him grow. It's funny what you learn about someone when they don't know they're being watched."

"He was sick," Nick said.

"You say *sick*. I saw a boy who had some of my tendencies, albeit he leaned toward younger females. Hunger is hunger and everybody needs to feed their appetite."

"You knew what he was? You knew he raped and sold young girls?"

"Raped, sold, and sometimes, when the need took him, killed young girls. If we're going to speak truths, Nick, then let's put it all on the table and leave nothing unsaid."

Nick watched the woman leering above him. She was enjoying this. It was the happiest he'd ever seen her in the short time he'd known her.

"That's right. A sick bastard. A pariah. And apparently just like his mom!" Nick spat the words.

"Easy, Nick. You've got the gist of where I'm going with this. I can finish explaining the details to Anaya without you around. So, watch your tone or you won't be around for the final act," Simmons said calmly.

Nick understood the veiled threat and didn't question its conviction. Her eyes told the tale and he knew he'd get no additional verbal shots without dire repercussions.

"Dear, sweet Anaya, your little Nick isn't the squeaky-clean G-man he's led you to believe." Simmons said. "He's got a dark side and my little Simon wasn't his first, but will probably be his last. Nick doesn't like to let the justice system run its course. Sometimes he plays judge, jury, and executioner."

Nick refused to look at Anaya, fearful at what judgement lay waiting.

"It's the latter that brought us together, Nick," Simmons teased.

Out of the corner of his eye, Nick felt Anaya's gaze, boring into him in search of some meaning to the madness. He ignored her, cocking his head and looking past Simmons at a blur of movement near the hallway.

"Don't worry I've been keeping track. Your secret's sa—"

Simmons stopped midsentence and her eyes widened. Her face contorted.

A loud bang accompanied the bright flash from the muzzle. And then silence.

Chapter 30

Nick lay flat, sprawled atop Spangler's dead body. Blood filled his eyes, causing him to blink uncontrollably. The automatic reaction told him he was alive. The thick salty liquid trickled past his lips and down into his mouth.

Nick spat, trying to vacate the foreign invasion before swallowing. He shoved hard against Simmons's small frame, freeing himself from the dead-body sandwich. He wiped hard to clear his face and eyes as best he could, smearing the warm wetness into his gray sweatshirt.

"Holy shit," Nick said, clearing his vision enough to see the rotund belly of Kemper Jones hovering above him.

"That's about the biggest understatement I've ever heard," Jones said, applying a thick layer of country twang.

Nick scrambled out of the twisted web of lifeless limbs and clamored to Anaya. Kneeling in front of her, he rubbed her hands and looked deep into her eyes. She seemed not to see him as she cast a vacant stare. He tugged the duct tape free from her mouth. Anaya winced as the adhesive worked hard to maintain its purchase on her skin.

"I'm so sorry, baby," Nick said, pulling free the last bit of bonded tape.

"Are you okay?" Anaya gasped.

Nick didn't answer because he wasn't sure. It wouldn't have been the first time he'd been too focused to notice a wound. He quickly patted himself down and gave her a nod of assurance.

"Got a knife?" Nick called over his shoulder to Jones.

"I'm a God-fearin' Texan. I'd be going against all that's good and holy if I didn't," Jones said, producing a folding knife from his front pants pocket and placing it into Nick's outstretched blood-covered palm.

Nick went to work releasing Anaya from each tight plastic restraint of the zip ties fastening her arms and legs to the chair. With the last one cut, Anaya fell forward. Nick reacted quickly, catching her gently in his arms. She sobbed quietly into his neck. The tears punctuated his failure to protect her as they trickled their path along his tainted skin. He failed to keep his promise to stay by her side at a time when she needed him most. That decision had left her alone and vulnerable to the reach of an incensed killer.

"I'm so sorry," Nick whispered.

"I tried to fight back. I tried to stop her from hurting me—from hurting our baby—" Anaya said, interspersed through ragged breaths.

"No. You shouldn't've had to do any of that. It's my fault." Nick's voice broke like a teenager hitting puberty. "I should've been there!"

"The baby! Oh my God no!" Anaya said, grasping at her stomach.

"What? Oh no—what did she do?" Nick pulled back to seek the answer in Anaya's face.

She said nothing. Nick tracked the gaze of Anaya's dark eyes down to Spangler's right hand and the willow branch he still held. Upon closer inspection, Nick realized that Spangler wasn't actually holding it, rather, he was held to it. The wider end of the cut tree limb was pressed tightly to the gloved palm of his hand, bound by several layers of black electrical tape.

"Have you got an ambulance coming?" Nick boomed the question at Jones.

"I called it in when I notified dispatch of my arrival. They're probably staged. I'll call 'em up."

Jones radioed for medical. Nick hadn't heard the sound until now. The wail of sirens punctuated Jones's radio transmission, and he heard heavy footsteps on the lower floor and the all-too-familiar squawk of police radios.

Nick pulled Anaya back into his tight embrace, trying desperately to calm her. The irregular jerking pattern of her body and rapidity of her breathing indicated that he was having little effect.

A small band of uniformed patrol officers from the Cedar Park Police Department filed quickly down the hallway toward the room. Nick looked on as Jones halted their movement at the doorway in an effort to hold the scene's integrity. Emergency medical personal were the only ones allowed entry.

For the second time in less than twenty-four hours he watched as Anaya was spirited away on a gurney with the life of his unborn child hanging in the balance. The thought of it caused his knees to buckle. Jones caught him by the arm, supporting his dead weight.

"I'll be right behind you!" Nick called out.

Anaya turned her head back toward him but said nothing as the squeaky-wheeled gurney clicked and clanged out of the door and down the hallway. Nick bore witness to the panic in her eyes, the effect of which was worsened by the opaque plastic of the portable oxygen mask covering the lower half of her face.

The short stocky Cedar Park detective initially assigned to the scene was more than happy to turn the investigation over to the combined investigative efforts of APD Homicide and the FBI.

"Well that was a first for me," Jones said, plopping heavily into a chair next to Nick.

"Huh?" Nick said in a daze.

"Turned over my gun. It feels weird. Like I did something wrong," Jones said, looking down at the worn leather of his unbuttoned holster, most of which was hidden under his ample love handle.

"You saved my life. And Anaya's. You did nothing wrong," Nick said, shifting his vacant stare from the tiled ground to his friend. The tangled bodies of Simmons and Spangler remained huddled in the center of the room, only twenty feet away.

"I know. Just feels weird is all."

"I'd like to say I know what you're feeling, but I've never—well not as a cop—pulled the trigger. Military—yes—but cop no," Nick said.

The two men sat in silence for several minutes.

Jones chuckled softly to himself. Nick looked at him expectantly, waiting for the punch line.

"I was just thinking," Jones said, still snickering.

"What could be so funny right now?" Nick asked.

"After spending a little time with her on that stakeout, I thought maybe I'd get the nerve to ask her out," Jones said.

"Simmons?" Nick asked.

"Yeah. I mean she was attractive and single. Best prospect I've had in quite some time," Jones said.

"You forgot the deranged serial killer part," Nick said, cracking a slight smile at the thought.

"Everybody's got their faults." Jones's chuckle erupted into a hearty laugh. "I wish I had winged her. Then maybe I could've visited her in prison."

"There's something seriously wrong with you my friend." Nick gave Jones a slap on the back.

"I wouldn't be able to do this job if there wasn't," Jones said.

Nick knew there was truth in that statement and nodded his agreement. *Maybe I'm too far gone? Maybe I'm closer to Simmons than a guy like Jones?* Nick thought, reflecting on Cheryl Simmons's exposure of his other side.

Anaya's screams filled the room and Nick jumped up from his seat. A robotic voice followed, "What bends but does not break? What weeps but does not cry?" Then followed by the loud crack of a whip. Another scream from Anaya and then the soft murmurs of her voice, "Please no more. My baby."

It abruptly ended, leaving Nick in a tragic state of utter delirium. He looked at Jones searching his face. Hoping his friend heard it too. Hoping he wasn't losing his mind.

Cavanaugh boomed from the other side of the room, "Sorry, I found it in her pocket."

Pete Cavanaugh walked toward Nick and Jones holding a small black remote.

"Looks like she had pre-recorded the events that took place in this room. It was set to play. So all she had to do was press this little button," Cavanaugh said.

"Jesus," Nick said, still coming down from the massive adrenaline dump of hearing Anaya's screams again.

"How are you two boys holding up?" Cavanaugh asked.

"Been better," Jones said.

"It was a clean shoot. Doesn't get much cleaner than that. Listen, you'll get a much-deserved two-week vacation while the paperwork gets sorted and then you'll be right back at it," Cavanaugh said.

"How about you? I know that Spangler was a friend of yours," Jones asked, looking up at the large Homicide detective.

"I'll deal. He was a good guy. A little odd, but a great guy. Did you know he collected PEZ dispensers? I guess that explained why he was still single," Cavanaugh said, injecting his dark humor on the situation.

"What else do you need from us?" Nick asked.

"We're about done with you guys for now. Luckily, I had some spare clothes in my trunk. Never know when I'm going to need a change out," Cavanaugh said.

Nick looked over at the brown paper evidence bags that held his blood-soaked clothing and then down at the oversized sweatshirt and jeans he was wearing. Over six feet tall with a muscular frame, Nick Lawrence would be considered big by most standards. But wearing Pete Cavanaugh's attire, he looked like a little boy playing dress up in daddy's clothes. The sight would have been almost comical if the setting wasn't so dire.

"I've got to go check on Anaya," Nick said.

"Get going. I'll reach out if I need anything more from you," Cavanaugh said, shaking Nick's hand before returning to the center of the room with the other detectives.

Nick paused, looking down at Jones who was absently rubbing his trigger finger. "I owe you my life."

Jones eyed his belly and chuckled. "You know how I'll take payment."

"I don't want to contribute to your early grave," Nick said.

"Well, then just find me a new girlfriend," Jones said.

Nick gave his friend a slap on his back and stepped to the threshold of the room. He stood next to the splintered frame of the door and glanced back at the two lifeless bodies, sprawled in the room's center.

Cheryl Simmons's hair was now a matted mess from the .40 caliber hollow point round that ripped through her skull. The bright fiery tendrils now tainted a dark sanguine color, denoting her tragic end. He turned to leave and hoped that his secrets would remain behind and die in that room, never to catch up to him again.

Chapter 31

The Emergency Room looked much like it did the night before. The world never seemed at a loss for tragedy. Each person's grief unique but the same. He did not envy the work of these doctors and nurses.

The receptionist, a kind-faced woman with wire rimmed glasses, kindly directed him to a seat in the waiting area. She'd told him that someone would be out to speak with him shortly. That was fifteen minutes ago and to Nick each passing second felt like hours.

A short balding man of Indian descent wearing a white lab coat over blue scrubs waddled out from the secured area. He paused to survey the crowd. He looked down at the tablet in his hand.

"Mr. Lawrence?"

Nick gave a wave of his hand and crossed the distance to the man quickly, almost at a run.

"Come with me," the doctor said curtly.

"How is she?" Nick asked desperately.

"She's in recovery."

"That's not what I asked." Nick made little effort to hide the intensity in his voice. His nerves were raw, and his anguish was exposed.

"She's going to be fine, Mr. Lawrence. No broken bones or long-term tissue damage," the doctor said, reading the notes from the digital chart as he walked.

"The baby?" Nick asked.

"I'm sorry."

"Sorry? What do you mean sorry?" Nick reeled.

"Mr. Lawrence, she lost the baby," the doctor said.

Nick stopped dead in his tracks. The hallway lights dimmed and brightened with each breath he took. He collapsed into the wall, sliding down into a heap on the glossy linoleum flooring. His stomach lurched, and he could barely suppress the urge to vomit.

Nick curled his arms tightly around his bent knees and rocked rhythmically.

The doctor's hand shook his shoulder. The words slowly penetrated his grief barrier. "She needs you. Mr. Lawrence, Anaya is going to need you to be strong."

She needs me? She needed me, and I wasn't there! She needed me, and I failed her! She needed me, and our baby is dead! Nick drowned himself in the despair of his thoughts.

Nick's mind screamed, but all that came out of his mouth was a mumbled, "You're right."

As if in a hypnotic trance, Nick rose. His eyes focused past the doctor to the endless row of doors that aligned the hallway. His face, stoic and calm, was a total contradiction to its contorted expression moments before.

"Lead the way," Nick said.

The doctor gave him a pitiful smile, turned and resumed his trek down the sterile confines of the hallway.

She lay half asleep in a room not much different from the one she'd been in the night before. Anaya looked peaceful, almost happy, but Nick knew this was most likely the aftershock from a sedative the doctor had given her after delivering the devastating news.

Their baby, never named, was now gone. The Ferryman's final victim claimed.

"Hey," Nick said softly, gently alerting her to his presence.

"Our baby's gone," Anaya whispered.

A single tear ran the tender curvatures of her face.

The knot in Nick's stomach constricted. He leaned in, kissing her cheek. The saltiness of the teardrop did little to quell his pain. If anything it amplified it.

A whimper gurgled up from his throat and he choked on the words. "I'm sorry."

Anaya said nothing. She turned her face away from his. Nick felt the icy dejection and understood. He failed her in a way that was unforgivable.

He gave her space, taking a seat beside her bed. The cheaply made cushion sounded its noisy protest to the infliction of Nick's weight.

Anaya shifted her body away toward the drawn blinds of the window.

Nick sobbed quietly, pressing his face into his hands, still tinged red with Simmons's blood. He only allowed himself a brief moment of self-pity before pushing it back into the deep recesses of his heart, the place where all his sadness lived in disharmony. To that place where the guilt of his brother's suicide now kept company with the failed promises to each of his dead parents. The remorse and grief for the death of his unborn child now added to its unbearable tonnage.

"I need time," Anaya said, still facing away.

"Time?" Nick sighed his resignation. "I understand. I'll be there for you regardless."

"You've said that before."

The words cut deep and he inhaled sharply at the pain of them. Nick exhaled, "Do you want me to leave?"

"Yes. I need to figure some things out," Anaya said.

He said nothing. The finality in her voice left him drained. He slid the chair back; the scraping of the wood on linoleum was louder than intended.

"I love you," Nick said.

Nothing. The silence that followed was louder than any scream she could've made.

Nick turned and walked out of the room, closing the door behind him. He stepped out into the busy thoroughfare of the hospital's hallway and drifted aimlessly away from the woman he loved, hopeful that someday he'd be allowed to return. Part of him very much doubted the likelihood.

Nick knew his past decisions had killed any chance of his family's future.

Chapter 32

    The tired springs of the bed creaked loudly as he adjusted, sitting up and positioning himself on its end. The yellow and beige floral pattern of the wallpaper blended seamlessly into the burnt umber threads of the gently worn fabric of the carpet. Nick had checked into the hotel, granting Anaya's request for space. That was two days ago but to him it was an eternity in his living purgatory.

    He wanted to be close enough if she needed him. So he chose to stay at the Sheraton in Georgetown, only a short drive away from their small home near the city's quaint town center. His selection in accommodations also served a secondary purpose. It was the same hotel where he'd shared an unbridled night of passion with Izzy.

On Saturday Nick had picked up the handle of Tito's Handmade Vodka, drowning himself in the clear spirit. The result of his homage to Izzy gave way to a challenging start to his Sunday.

It was already well past noon and Nick had only made it as far as the edge of the bed. His head pounded and what little light that managed to slip through the gap in the curtain cut into his brain like a laser beam used by a sadistic James Bond villain.

Nick checked his phone. He'd missed several calls but none of them were from Anaya. If it wasn't Anaya, then he didn't care. He let the phone slip from his hands to the floor and stood. Nick slogged his way to the sink and ran cold water from the faucet.

Bent over the white porcelain basin, Nick splashed his face repeatedly, trying to wash away the throbbing that arced across his forehead. He stuck his mouth down by the spout, slurping at the waterfall in a desperate attempt to rehydrate.

He didn't hear it at first, but the sound became clearer as he rose up. Water dripped profusely from his tired face. The three quick successive raps at the door seemed louder in his current physical state.

Nick turned, surveying the mess of clothes and food wrappers. Three more bangs, this time louder than before.

"Coming!" Nick yelled. The sound of his voice resonated with dizzying effect and his stomach lurched in protest.

The knock came again, this time quicker and louder than before.

"I said I'm coming for God's sake!" Nick said, trying to speak forcefully while at the same time maintaining a low volume.

Nick flicked free the chain lock and it fell alongside the metal frame of the door, swinging noisily as he yanked hard, pulling the door open. Nick kept his left hand on the handle for balance and used his other to shield his eyes from the bright light pouring in from the hallway.

"Well, you look like dog shit in the hot sun!" Declan boomed.

Nick furrowed his brow at the sight of his friend, confused by his arrival and worried that he'd lost his mind or was having some weird vodka-induced dream.

"Nice to see you too. Aren't you going to invite me in?" Declan asked.

Nick stepped back from the doorway allowing his friend access.

Declan chuckled softly, stepping over an opened pizza box containing a boneyard of crust. "I see that you're doing well."

"I thought—Ohio... weren't you on an op?" Nick asked, perplexed.

"I was. Not the massive compound ATF thought it was. Big surprise there. Turned out to be just a handful of rednecks with a couple guns. You should've seen how they about pissed themselves when we popped out of the bushes on 'em," Declan said, smiling.

"I'm still not tracking. You flew here? Why?" Nick mumbled.

"I told you when we last talked that we needed to give Izzy a proper send-off," Declan said, picking up the near-empty bottle. "Looks like you got yourself a head start."

The thought of drinking anything, let alone vodka, made the room spin. Nick fought hard to keep from throwing up on his friend.

"Shower up and let's get the hair of the dog in you," Declan said, pushing Nick's shoulder and guiding him toward the bathroom.

Nick grunted but didn't resist, using the momentum of Declan's shove to assist his feeble progression.

The shower felt good, revitalizing him enough to feel a modicum of functionality. Nick stepped out of the bathroom; beads of water followed the lines cut by his rugged physique ending at the white curled lip of the hotel towel wrapped tightly around his waist. Declan stood holding two plastic cups. About one finger's worth of the clear liquid swished at the bottom as Declan leveled one cup in his direction.

"Shit, this is going to hurt," Nick mumbled.

"To Izzy," Declan said.

At that, Nick accepted the cup without further hesitation. The two raised their cups.

"To Izzy," Nick said.

The two friends tapped the plastic cups together. Nick's voice broke at the mention of her name, but the burn of the micro-distilled spirit masked his pain.

"Neither one of us would be alive to raise this glass had she not been there for us," Declan said, pouring the drink down his throat.

Both men's eyes watered slightly, embracing the silent solidarity that could only be understood by them.

Declan cleared his throat and placed the cup down on a nearby dresser. "There's another reason I'm here."

Nick saw something in his friend's eye. A nervous discomfort he'd not seen before.

"What's up?" Nick asked.

"Simmons."

The mention of her name sent a shockwave of rage through Nick's body, causing his hands to begin involuntarily shaking. "What about her?"

"She had a backup plan for you."

"Backup plan? What the hell are you talking about?" Nick asked.

"I guess she wanted a fail-safe in the event that you managed to stop her," Declan said. His voice was uncharacteristically softer.

"I'm still not following you."

"The murders, Nick. Montrose and his crew. Others too. She had a detailed file. Really detailed," Declan said, breaking eye contact.

Nick exhaled slowly. His mind reeling at the exposure of his past, compounded further by his unrelenting hangover.

"A mutual friend of ours got wind of it and tipped me off. I wanted to be here when they came for you. I called in some favors and had them wait until I got here. I wanted to show you that I've still got your back," Declan said.

"When they come for me? Who?" Nick asked frantically.

"Us. The Bureau. They've got an arrest warrant for you. I've been given a small window of time to speak with you. I told them that we would walk out together," Declan said.

"You're here to arrest me?" Nick asked, dropping heavily to a seated position on the end of the bed.

"I'm here to help an old friend—my best friend—get through a terrible situation," Declan said.

"Jesus," Nick hissed.

"We'll figure it out. Promise. I don't know how, but we'll find our way out of this. Guys like us always find a way," Declan said.

"You keep saying we. I'm pretty sure you dodged the bullet on *your* federal case," Nick said sarcastically.

"I had no say in this. I was worried that it might go badly if someone else came for you," Declan said.

"Badly?"

"You've lost everything over the last few days and when I heard about this arrest coming down, I seriously didn't know if you could handle it," Declan said compassionately.

Nick's head drooped low as if the muscles in his neck could no longer support its burdensome weight.

"Let's get it over with," Nick said, resigned.

Declan walked over to the round coffee table and retrieved Nick's duty weapon. Nick watched as his friend removed the magazine and emptied the chamber before dropping it into the cargo pocket on his left side.

Nick dressed quickly without giving any thought to his attire, knowing that soon the only wardrobe would be that provided by his awaiting correctional facility. He turned to face his friend. Nick's expression was flat; every ounce of emotional energy had been completely depleted. The two men embraced, exchanging hearty backslaps.

"I'll figure something out. This isn't the end," Declan said gritting his teeth.

Nick said nothing.

Nick followed Declan's lead. The door opened and they were greeted by several agents. Two of them had their pistols out of the holster and bootlegged against their thighs. A third stood behind them, swaying nervously and palming a pair of hinge cuffs. It took a second for Nick to recognize the man. Gary Salazar, his rookie chauffer from his ride back from the airport, stood awkwardly in the backdrop preparing to make the arrest, probably the first arrest of his career.

Nick turned slowly and placed his hands at the small of his back. Each click of the cuff's ratchets were like nails banging into his coffin. He was being buried alive, entombed by the dark secrets brought to light. His need to right injustice now left him a victim of his own righteousness.

Nick walked into the pale light of day under the escort of men who used to serve by his side, crossing over that invisible dividing line. The condemnation of his actions weighed heavily. Nick knew the justice system better than most. It would not be kind to him. He'd always prepared for the worst and hoped for the best, but this time he was caught off guard.

His future had been stolen by his past, and what lay ahead was uncharted territory.

Thank you for reading!

I look forward to hearing from readers. Please feel free to email me: info@brianchristophershea.com

Connect with me on social media:
Facebook:
www.facebook.com/thecamelsbackbook
Instagram:
www.instagram.com/brianchristophershea
Twitter:
twitter.com/BrianCShea

Be on the lookout for book 4:
THE WOLF'S DOOR.
Anticipated release in early March!

https://brianchristophershea.com

Made in the USA
Middletown, DE
27 November 2018